TOOLS OF THE TRADE

by

Geoff Collins

TOOLS OF THE TRADE

The publisher does not have any control over and does not assume any responsibility for author or third-party websites or their content.

Front cover designed by Erik Johnson
www.robertlangestudios.com/erik-johnson/

Cover art:
Copyright © Shutterstock_232648147_CHAIWATPHOTOS

Back cover art:
Copyright © Shutterstock_259134722_Laboko

Interior art:
Fish Hook original art by KC Collins
Copyright © Shutterstock_259134722_Laboko

Edited by Joe Gartrell and Ben Gibson of Word Mule.
www.wordmule.com

Published by A & J Publishing, LLC
3266 Hartwell Street
Johns Island, SC 29455

Visit the author website: www.booksbycollins.com

Categories: FICTION/Thrillers Crime

ISBN: 978-1-948046-31-2 (eBook),
ISBN: 978-1-948046-32-9 (paperback)

Version 2018.09.25

To my friends at Project Paw Alive and the many other police and military K-9 organizations and support groups.

Protecting the K-9s Who Protect Us

Project Paws Alive Inc. is a 501c3 nonprofit organization dedicated to providing K-9 stab and bulletproof vests and other vital K-9 protective equipment to underfunded Law Enforcement, Fire, Search and Rescue and Military K-9 units nationwide.

Donations can be made at Projectpawsalive.org or by mail.

Project Paws Alive Inc.
1193 Southeast Port St. Lucie Boulevard
Suite 289
Port Saint Lucie, FL 34952

A special thanks to Joe Gartrell and Ben Gibson of Word Mule.
www.wordmule.com

&

Erik Johnson
www.robertlangestudios.com/erik-johnson/

*"The justifications of men who kill should always be heard
with skepticism, said the monster."*
–Patrick Ness, *A Monster Calls*

*"When the Fox hears the Rabbit scream he comes a-runnin',
but not to help."*
–Thomas Harris, *The Silence of the Lambs*

THE TOOLS OF THE TRADE

CHAPTER ONE

HE LOOKED LIKE a lawyer. Wearing one of his many $3,000 virgin wool Armani suits, Phillip Bryson was pushing fifty, his jet-black hair showing only a touch of gray. At a shade over six feet tall, he carried himself with a confidence born of privilege. Bryson's driver eased the black Cadillac Escalade to the curb in front of Antonio's Bar at the corner of Bay and Erie in Jersey City. Bryson snapped shut the Bosca attaché resting next to him, leaned forward, and said, "Thank you, Isaac, I should only be about twenty minutes."

Housed in a two-story building with the main bar on the ground floor and a small social club above it, Antonio's looked like a thousand other neighborhood watering holes. From the black metal door to the block glass window to the nondescript charcoal gray brick exterior, it was the kind of place meant to shrug off unwanted attention.

Bryson exited the Escalade and entered the bar, pausing a moment to allow his eyes to adjust to the dim light. The inside of Antonio's was actually quite nice, with a long, polished mahogany bar complete with brass foot rails. A large backlit mirror with three rows of liquor bottles ran against the left wall behind the bar. Phillip recognized the two foot soldiers sitting at the bar nursing drinks. They seemed to take no notice of him, but there was a slight bulge under their sport coats—a clear indication both men were carrying.

The walls were covered with framed and autographed black-and-white photos of actors, singers, and other pseudo-celebrities who'd visited Antonio's over the years. A muted television mounted on the wall at the far end of the bar showed a European soccer game. An open area in the rear of the room contained eight tables covered with red-checkered tablecloths and wine bottle candles. The place had a comfortable, neighborhood feel.

A rather rotund, gray-haired bartender who looked to be as wide as he was tall aimlessly wiped down the bar. Bryson nodded to him. The bartender returned the nod and lifted his head slightly, confirming he was expected upstairs. Phillip headed directly to the rear staircase.

The second-floor social club had the distinct smell of cigars and fine leather. Phillip found Mario Rossini and Salvatore "Sal" Ruggiero seated at a bare card table, their eyes fixed on a large flat-screen—CNN was airing some not especially newsworthy "breaking news." As soon as Bryson entered the room, Ruggiero, the younger of the two men, grabbed the remote and shut off the TV.

Ruggiero was a big man whose job was to insulate Mr. Rossini from any direct connection to the family's business. He was tough, quick-tempered and fiercely loyal to Rossini. In the hierarchy of organized crime, Sal was the caporegime, the capo. He reported directly to Rossini, one of the organization's underbosses. Rossini was responsible for the family's business operations in the Southeast part of the country and reported directly to Liborio "Barney" Bellomo, the head of the Genovese family.

Rossini had just been booked and charged with racketeering under the RICO statute. He had been arraigned the previous week and was now out on bail.

Phillip took a seat and nodded to Rossini, who returned the nod. After almost fifteen years of representing Rossini, Phillip knew Mario rarely bothered with small talk. He got right to it. "My contacts in the U.S. Attorney's Office tell me they're looking to connect you with the recent unpleasant situation in Charleston. They're in the process of gathering evidence from people down there."

"What do they have?" Rossini asked.

"Not much beyond some circumstantial evidence, but I'm concerned with what they may uncover in Charleston. They've got Angelo Vitale in a federal prison down there. Any way he could connect you to Charleston?"

Even though the question was directed to Rossini, Ruggiero answered, "The whole fucking thing is a piece of shit. The good news is that DiMarco and Grasso were the only real ties to Mario, and they're both dead. Mario's moving everybody around and bringing in some help from Atlanta so that we don't start missing shipments while the competition smells blood in the water. Like I said, they got Vitale in solitary, so we can't get to him like we did DiMarco."

Phillip raised both hands, interrupting Ruggiero. "Sal, my only concern is how to legally protect Mario and his businesses. The less I know about what you can and can't do to Vitale in prison the better. Now, my question was a simple one. Is there anyone else in Charleston we need to worry about?"

Ruggiero's nostrils flared—he didn't abide lectures well. "I was getting to that before you interrupted me. DiMarco and Grasso were the only two who had any direct contact. And like I said, they're both dead. There's no doubt Vitale knows our businesses down there, but he was just a soldier. He never had any direct contact with Mario. But we still may have a problem."

Now Rossini spoke up. "What problem?"

"It's that geek, Allen Miller. He's the one who hacked into the hospital computer system and blew the lid off DiMarco's hustle in the first place. Plus, Miller's secretary and a few of his friends were involved in busting up the hospital thing and exposing some of our other operations."

"So, what do we know about Miller and his friends?" Rossini asked.

"According to my contact, the Feds took over. Local cops are pretty much out of the picture now," Sal answered. "But I did get names."

Sal removed a small notepad from his pocket and flipped through the pages. "Secretary's name is Sarah Pryor. There's also a guy that runs a dog training business named Nick Giordano and two guys working for him. The two guys are ex-Army, but I didn't get their names."

"Sal," Rossini said, "get ahold of your cop contact. I need to know how much this Miller guy really knows and if he can connect any of it to me. Same goes for his secretary and the dog guy."

Bryson stood. "Gentlemen, I believe this is a good time for me to leave." Bryson nodded to Ruggiero and then turned to Mario and continued, "I'll let you know as soon as I have something new on the case."

Mr. Rossini waited until Bryson left and the door was shut. "All right, Sal. Bellomo wants someone down there in case those people need to be taken care of."

"Who's doin' the job?"

"Carlo Tucci."

Ruggiero raised his eyebrows. "Jesus, Mario," he said. "They must be serious about this shit."

CHAPTER TWO

IT HAD BEEN several weeks since Phillip Bryson met Mario Rossini and Sal Ruggiero at Antonio's to discuss the RICO charges being brought against Mario. Ruggiero had just finished his plate of risotto with grilled pork and was washing it down with his second glass of Toscana Rosso when Carlo Tucci entered the bar. The two embraced. *"Bello vederti amico mio!"* Sal said. "Come with me and we'll talk."

Sal poured two cups of coffee and led Tucci upstairs, where they could speak in private. As the two settled in, Sal added a bit of sambuca to their coffees.

~~~

Carlo Tucci was an enforcer. He was in his late fifties and had been a made man for more than twenty-five years. At six feet and 235 pounds, he was a bull. But he wasn't your stereotypical
~~~

knuckle-dragging enforcer like Joseph "The Animal" Barbosa, Giovanni Brusca, and "Sammy the Bull" Gravano—all of whom were legends due to their ostentatious personalities. Tucci was a quiet man. He lived in the shadows. But few were more adept with the "tools of the trade" than Carlo Tucci.

He was born in Brooklyn Heights in 1958. His father, Piero Tucci, was an illiterate Italian immigrant who worked on the waterfront docks in Lower Manhattan until his death in 1969.

Back in the 1950s, life on the docks could have been taken straight from a scene in *On the Waterfront*. Piero fought to make a living amid the corruption—if you wanted to work, you had to kick-back part of your wages to the bosses and turn a blind eye to the mob's activities. The mob bosses made use of the workers' desperation, to steal entire shipments of cargo and intimidate unions into giving them lucrative shipping contracts. By the late 1950s, the Genovese family had taken control of the waterfront on the southern side of Manhattan.

Carlo was only eleven when his father died. He and his mother, Emilia, struggled to survive on the drug and crime-infested streets of the city. Emilia did her best, but work was hard to find during the economic and social turmoil of the early 1970s. Emilia and Carlo found themselves homeless at times and were forced to find shelter in one of the hundreds of boarded-up, abandoned buildings on the Lower East Side.

Carlo turned to panhandling and petty theft until he was old enough to find work on the same docks where his father had toiled. He eventually caught the eye of Vincent "The Chin"

Gigante, a powerful member of the Genovese crime family. Carlo was brought into the organization as a waterfront "debt collector." After a few years, Carlo became an associate in the mob and ran a crew that collected protection payoffs from merchants at the Fulton Fish Market. At age thirty-three, Carlo Tucci "made his bones" by carrying out his first contract killing.

A few months later, he received a phone call from Vincent Gigante and was instructed to put on a suit and prepare to be collected. His time had come. Vincent Gigante was sponsoring Carlo Tucci to become a made man in the Genovese family.

The ceremony began with Gigante cutting Carlo's trigger finger and letting his blood drip onto a picture of the Virgin Mary. The picture was then crumpled, put into Carlo's hands, and set ablaze. The picture burned in his hands while the "oath of Omerta"—the code of silence—was given. The code forbids a made man, no matter the circumstances, from ratting to the authorities. Breaking the code meant death.

Carlo was Gigante's bodyguard until 1997, when Gigante was tried and convicted of racketeering and murder. He was sent to prison, where he died in 2005 at the age of seventy-seven.

While it never came to light, Carlo Tucci was involved in all ten Gigante-sanctioned hits. After Gigante's imprisonment, Carlo could have moved up in the organization but chose to remain behind the scenes, surreptitiously serving his bosses.

Carlo Tucci's life was anything but the prototypical Hollywood image of a mobster swaggering around in flashy cars, wearing expensive tailored suits and diamond rings on his pinky finger. Tucci married his wife, Susan, in the late '80s and moved into an unpretentious three-bedroom home in Brooklyn Heights, where they raised their daughter, Sofia. His wife died in 2013 from lung cancer.

When Sofia was seven years old, she contracted bacterial meningitis—resulting in complete hearing loss. Sofia was now grown and living with her father in the same small Brooklyn Heights home he bought in 1988. While Sofia could speak, she was self-conscious about it and preferred to communicate by signing. Carlo obviously became proficient in the use of sign language.

Sofia knew that her father had once been involved with organized crime, but she didn't know a thing about the murders he'd carried out over the years. Carlo was extremely protective of Sofia and made every effort to insulate her from his "other life." She believed her "Papa" had moved away from that world and now lived the quiet life of a part-time butcher at a small grocery store in Brooklyn.

Carlo's life was interrupted periodically when his "special talents" were needed by the mob to "fix" certain situations. While Carlo's life could be considered somwhat prosaic, his low profile served him well, whether he was required to convince someone to do his bosses' bidding or "solve" situations in a more permanent fashion. By 2017, Carlo had commited or been involved in some fifteen mob assassinations. Amazingly, nothing was ever pinned on him. His modest, inconspicuous lifestyle and meticulous planning kept him protected.

~~~

After a few innocuous questions about Carlo's daughter, Sal got down to business. "We have a situation."

Carlo simply nodded.

"New York wants you down in Charleston." He then explained what had happened at Mercy General Hospital and the possible unmasking of the syndicate's Charleston operations. "The Feds are trying to connect what happened down there with our people here in Jersey. Danny Santo is getting what's left of the operation there reorganized. New York wants Frank Petrelli moved into Charleston from Atlanta. He'll clean our money through Orlando until Santo sets up another front company in Charleston. DiMarco has been taken care of, but we believe there are a few civilians down there that may know too much. Get familiar with these people. Once we learn how much they know, we'll let you know how we want it handled."

Sal explained that his police contacts had given Petrelli what information they've got on Miller and his friends. "When you get to Charleston, get ahold of Petrelli. He'll give you what he's got on these people."

Sal ended the meeting by passing Carlo an envelope containing a forged driver's license and credit card, as well as $3,000 to cover his expenses in Charleston.

Carlo worked his regular shift that afternoon at the grocery store. When he clocked out, he let his manager know he'd be out for the next few weeks attending to his elderly mother who
~~~

lived by herself upstate in Webster, New York. Carlo's manager was always understanding when he needed periodic time off to deal with his mother's situation. His mother, though, did not live in Webster—or anywhere else for that matter. She'd died in 1984.

Carlo packed two suitcases the following morning. The first contained clothes, toiletries, his computer, and some reading material. The second was quite a bit heavier than the first. It included a variety of items that could be referred to as the tools of his trade.

Unbeknownst to Ruggiero, Carlo had met secretly with Liborio Bellomo the previous week. Bellomo had given him two "burner" phones and an additional job to do once he arrived in Charleston. Carlo put one of the burners in the heavier suitcase and slid the other in his pants pocket.

He left at 9:00 a.m. that morning, driving about eight and a half hours down I-95 to just inside the North Carolina border. He spent the night at a Ramada Inn. The following morning, he made the five-hour drive to Charleston, arriving early that afternoon. He checked into a Best Western on Savannah Highway before heading out to meet Petrelli at a small beachfront villa on the Isle of Palms. Max DiMarco had purchased the property a few years earlier through one of his shell companies. It was used to both entertain and house his associates during visits to Charleston.

The two men had worked together in New York before Petrelli was sent to Atlanta to oversee business in Georgia. There was no love lost between the two. Petrelli was a small man with a complexion like a mushroom—the kind that is more gray than white. He thought of himself as Joe Pesci's character from *Goodfellas*, but everyone else referred to him as "The Weasel" because of his thin face, pointed nose, and small, beady eyes. He drank too much, played the horses, and had a weakness for the ladies. He'd become an embarrassment to his bosses. He was both ruthless and reckless—a dangerous combination for the family business. Carlo knew that Petrelli and his indiscretions would soon be dealt with.

Carlo didn't think Frank deserved the level of responsibility he'd been given, but Petrelli had the benefit of nepotism. He was the cousin of Gino Santangelo, an upper-level lieutenant in the Genovese family. He'd never have risen to his current position had it not been for his cousin. To Carlo, Petrelli was like that annoying itch in the middle of your back you couldn't quite reach. The guy was a world-class jerk.

Carlo arrived at the villa at about 8:00 p.m. that evening. Petrelli met him at the door dressed in a paisley swimsuit that looked to be a few sizes too big. He had a drink in his hand— obviously not his first. Frank offered Carlo a drink, but he declined.

"Tell me what you got," Carlo said, not wanting to stay any longer than necessary.

"Great to see you, too, old pal," Petrelli said. He downed his drink and poured another and then spent the next fifteen minutes giving Carlo every piece of information the police informants had gathered.

Carlo sat quietly as Petrelli refilled his drink and said, "Listen, Tucci, I'm here to make sure the money moves to Orlando until Santo gets his act together. Can't wait to get my ass back to Atlanta. I got no time for whatever the fuck you're doin' down here. So whatever it is, handle it yourself." That was just fine with Carlo. He would handle the job by himself, keeping only Mr. Bellomo and Mario Rossini appraised of his progress.

Carlo Tucci spent the next week familiarizing himself with the lay of the land as it pertained to Allen Miller, Nick Giordano, and the others who were thought to have exposed DiMarco's businesses. He was at the ready to dip into his second suitcase and take care of any problems that needed to be eliminated. No one other than Liborio Bellomo and Mario Rossini were aware of the second reason Carlo Tucci had been sent to Charleston—one that would involve Frank Petrelli and become clear as events unfolded.

CHAPTER THREE

ALLEN MILLER LEFT his newly renovated Bee Street condo in downtown Charleston and headed to the coffee shop affectionately known as "The Cup." Born into elite Charleston society, he might have been surprised to learn that Jersey mobsters were now combing through his years at MIT, his five-year career at the Department of Homeland Security, and his company, CyberNet Security.

It had been several weeks since Allen had been to The Cup. His most recent assignment had landed him in the hospital after being kidnapped and nearly beaten to death by some Charleston thugs who were working for a crime syndicate out of New Jersey. A close family friend had hired Allen to investigate what he believed to be the theft of narcotics from Charleston's Mercy General Hospital. His computer expertise, along with the tireless work of his assistant, Sarah Pryor, allowed Allen to penetrate the hospital's computer system and discover how the drugs were stolen. This discovery led to a network of more sinister criminal activities run by a man named Max DiMarco. DiMarco had headed up the Charleston arm of the New Jersey syndicate until he was assassinated in prison.

If it hadn't been for his friends Nick Giordano, Josh Taylor, and Zach Brown, Allen wouldn't be alive today. The three of them saved Allen's life after he was kidnapped by DiMarco's men and taken to a small warehouse in North Charleston. In addition to saving Allen's life, his friends killed two of DiMarco's crew and helped the police arrest both DiMarco and one of his associates named Angel Vitale. With the threat of several RICO indictments facing them, both DiMarco and Vitale agreed to a deal in exchange for testifying against Mario Rossini, one of the main mob bosses in the syndicate. Both had been promised entry into the U.S. Department of Justice witness protection program. They were transferred to a federal prison in Estill, South Carolina, and would be held there until their testimony was required. Shortly after they arrived at the prison, Max DiMarco was found dead in one of the shower rooms, his throat slit. The Justice Department immediately transferred Vitale to solitary confinement. The move was not only for his own protection but also, more importantly, to secure his ability to testify against members of the New Jersey crime syndicate.

Nick Giordano and Angela Martin were waiting for Allen when he walked into The Cup. Nick owned a police dog training business called the Lowcountry Police Dog Academy out on Johns Island, and Angela worked as an emergency room nurse at Mercy General Hospital.

A broad smile spread across Nick's face as he shook Allen's hand. Angela gave him a warm hug, Allen wincing at the sharp pain he felt from his bruised ribs.

"Well," Nick said, "look who rejoined the living. Angela, help this patient to a table while I get him a coffee."

Just over five feet, two inches tall and only a few pounds over a hundred soaking wet, Angela was one tough lady. She'd grown up with her mom in North Charleston's Union Heights neighborhood—one of the roughest and most crime-infested areas in the city.

Dressed in her navy blue scrubs, she took Allen's arm and led him to one of the tables in the back corner of the coffee shop. The multiple bruises and cuts on Allen's face and legs were healing nicely, but it would be a while before his bruised ribs would return to normal.

After they were seated, Angela patted his hand and said, "God, it's good to see you. When did you get back to your condo?"

"Just last night," Allen said. "Mom and Dad kept me prisoner at their place 'til they thought I looked presentable enough to show my face in public. I'm anxious to get back to the office and catch up. Sarah's been holding down the fort."

Angela said, "My Zach keeps asking about you, and so does everyone else out at the Academy."

Allen said, "I owe those guys big time."

Nick made it back to the table, gave Allen his coffee, and sat down. "So, what's new in your world?"

"Well," said Allen, "I got a call from a lawyer at the Federal Court in New Jersey, and he's flying in this week to talk to me. He said he also wants to see you, Josh, and Zach. I gave him your business number, so I'd expect he'll contact you pretty soon. The guy's name is Stanley Scott."

"That's fine," said Nick. "We're just all glad you're back and feeling better. That Westcott shit sure was a dump truck full of crazy. Anyway, you look like you're recovering nicely. Oh, by the way, I just got a heads-up that Homeland Security is going to come through on their promise for another six sniffers. It's a good excuse to have everyone out to the Academy for another cookout this Sunday. Amy and Angela are coming. You feel up to it?"

"That would be great. I've been cooped up for long enough. Plus, I'd really like to personally thank Josh and Zach for what they did. Would it be okay if I invited Sarah and her husband? After what happened, she feels like she knows all of you."

"Absolutely," said Nick.

Angela stood and said, "I gotta get to work, boys." She bent down and gave Allen a peck on his cheek. "Now, don't you be gettin' mixed up with any more bad dudes, sweetheart. I'll catch you two later."

Nick and Allen talked for another ten minutes or so, with Allen explaining that the U.S. Attorney told him RICO charges have been filed against one of the Mafia bosses in New Jersey. "The guy's name is Rossini, and he supposed to be connected to DiMarco's organization here."

Nick, like Allen, lived right around the corner from The Cup on the sixth floor of the Bee Street condos—close to the sprawling MUSC complex and Mercy General Hospital. He'd rented a one-bedroom loft condo there.

Nick had moved into his place about five years ago, when he returned to Charleston after spending a year on his dad's peach farm in Killian, South Carolina.

His life was forever changed late one August night in 2010 when he and his police dog, Max, were staking out a suspected crack house in North Charleston. The drug bust went terribly wrong and ended in the death of the dealer, a fellow officer, and Nick's dog. Nick was shot in the chest and right knee. The doctors at MUSC's Trauma Unit were able to save his leg, but the damage was so severe he would never regain full use of his leg; the pain was a constant reminder of the deaths he believed he was responsible for.

At first, the drinking helped ease the constant pain in his leg and numb the emotional anxiety building inside him. The drinking got worse, and he started to show up late for work—at times missing it altogether. He was drowning in self-pity and felt he'd fallen so deep into the muck he might never get out.

Finally, in August 2011, he came to terms with the downward spiral his life had taken. Nick loved being a cop, but now it was clear that the booze and the guilt were ripping his world apart. He thought staying on the force was a way to honor the memory of his friend whose life he felt he'd cut short, but it just wasn't working. The following week, Nick submitted his formal resignation from the force, packed a bag, and made the two-hour drive north to his dad's peach farm in Killian. Nick's dad, Robert, had worked his small peach farm for the past forty years, the last ten without his wife, Gloria, who lost her battle with breast cancer back in 2001.

The year with his dad back home in Killian was great for Nick, not only physically but also mentally. It was a long process, but with the help of his dad and months of therapy sessions with Dr. Judy Bailey, Nick was able to begin the process of forgiving himself for what he'd done the night of the shooting. He began to regain control of his life. He still walked with a limp and the nightmares had not completely disappeared, but he'd recovered to the point that he was able to consider leaving the safety of the farm.

With the help of his dad and his K-9 ex-boss, Lieutenant Steve Williams, Nick was able to start his own company, the Lowcountry Police Dog Academy. The land was bought, fencing installed, a dozen kennels constructed, necessary training equipment purchased, and the initial batch of German Shepherds delivered to the Academy within the first three and a half months.

Over the next five years, Nick's reputation grew, and his business continued to expand. Soon he was getting orders for "Nick Giordano–trained" police dogs from North Carolina and Georgia in addition to South Carolina. By 2017, his company had five employees and a backlog of orders. Despite his success, he'd never forgotten the depths to which he'd fallen, and the people who had helped him regain his life. Nick Giordano would never again take anything for granted.

Nick and Allen left The Cup together. Allen headed to his Queen Street office, and Nick made the twenty-five-minute drive to the Academy on Johns Island. He pulled his 2013 Toyota truck into the parking lot in front of the modified mobile home that acted as the company's office.

The Academy covered three acres. Off to the left were the original twelve kennels housing the German Shepherds in training. The actual training area—an open field with a variety of wooden hoops, ladders, ramps, and jumps—was located behind the office and covered the majority of the facility. Another eight-unit kennel had recently been built in the rear of the grounds to house dogs ordered by the Department of Homeland Security.

His trainers, Josh Taylor and Zach Brown, were working two of the dogs in the field and waved to Nick. Nick's secretary, Sally Reed, had just hung up the phone when Nick entered the office.

"Morning, Sally," said Nick.

"Good morning to you," she said, handing him a stack of messages. "You just got a call from a Stanley Scott. He's a lawyer at the U.S. Attorney's Office in New Jersey. He wanted you to call him back as soon as you got in."

"Thanks, I was expecting the call. Can you grab the paperwork on the TSA dogs Zach's working with?"

He glanced at the attorney's message as he entered his office, thinking about how lucky he was to have Sally. She joined him just as he was getting the business started, and he didn't know what he would do without her. Sally handled purchasing, invoicing, payroll, taxes, and just about everything else, with the exception of actually training the dogs. She'd never been married and was very protective of Nick.

Once seated at his desk, Nick grabbed his phone and punched in the number for Stanley Scott. His call was answered by what he assumed to be Scott's secretary. Nick identified himself and told her he was returning Mr. Scott's call.

A moment later, Scott was on the line. "Mr. Giordano, thank you for getting back to me so quickly."

"No problem, sir. What can I do for you?"

"I'm one of the attorneys working in the Department of Justice's New Jersey District. We're looking into an individual by the name of Mario Rossini. I understand you were one of the individuals involved in the apprehension of Max DiMarco and his associate, Angelo Vitale."

"Yes, two of my employees and I were part of that."

"Mr. DiMarco and Mr. Vitale worked for Mr. Rossini," Scott said, "and I'd like to talk to you about them. I'm scheduled to meet Allen Miller this Thursday and would like you and your two employees at that meeting."

"That's no problem," Nick said. "Just let me know when and where, and we'll be there."

"Great. My assistant and I are flying into Charleston Thursday morning, and we have a conference room reserved at the Hilton near the airport. I'd like to meet with all of you folks there at 11:30 that morning."

"That'll work. Do you need us to bring anything to the meeting?"

"No, I don't believe so. I appreciate your help on this and look forward to meeting you."

"Thank you, sir. We'll see you Thursday at 11:30."

After hanging up, Nick made a few more calls and then headed outside to check in with Josh and Zach. Nick was leaving the office when Sally said, "Oh, I almost forgot. Amy called this morning to remind you to meet her at six for dinner tonight at AC's."

"Thanks, Sally. Got it."

She gave Nick a sly smile and said, "Amy's a sweetheart. You take care of that girl. She's definitely a keeper!"

Amy Anderson had worked at The Coffee Cup for the last seven months. She'd gone through a difficult divorce about two years before. Her ex was a lawyer. Setting all the lawyer jokes aside, this guy really was the proverbial asshole. There'd been some physical and mental abuse, and she was lucky she got out of the marriage when she did. Amy said she'd "edited" those years out of her life—she thought that sounded poetic. After the divorce, she'd walked away with virtually nothing, and at thirty, she was back in school working on a teaching degree at the College of Charleston.

Nick had a few relationships since returning to Charleston after spending the year with his dad in Killian, but none of them developed into anything serious. The demands of starting and running a successful business left Nick little time for much of a social life. He and Amy had started to date about three months ago. Both of them had weathered dark times in their lives and had grown extremely close over the short time they had been together.

CHAPTER FOUR

CHARLESTON HAD BEEN hit with an unusual heatwave. As soon as Nick left his air-conditioned office, he could feel the heat and humidity building despite it being mid-October. Josh Taylor and Zach Brown were working with two dogs being trained in narcotic detection for the Transportation Security Administration (TSA). The increased terrorist threat made it difficult for the DHS to keep up with the demand of professionally trained dogs. Through the help of Nick's ex-boss and friend, Steve Williams, the Academy had received an order for six narcotic sniffers two months ago. Homeland Security promised an additional order if the dogs could be fully trained and delivered in eight weeks.

Nick couldn't help but smile as he watched Josh and Zach work the dogs. Josh Taylor had been with the company since shortly after it started. He maintained his close-cropped military haircut, and despite his small stature, he was the kind of guy you'd want next to you, whether it was a firefight in Afghanistan or a bar fight in North Charleston.

Zach Brown was a huge man. At six-foot-five and 250 pounds, his shaved black head glistened with sweat, and his black Army boots, jeans, and T-shirt were a little worse for wear since Nick hired him three months ago. Both Josh and Zach had returned to the States after multiple tours of duty in Iraq and Afghanistan.

Like many men and women returning from combat, both found it difficult to adjust to civilian life and suffered severe bouts of PTSD. However, intensive counselling and VA peer group support had allowed them to deal with their disability and move on with their lives.

Nick had brought two bottles of water with him and continued to watch Josh and Zach work the dogs until they took a break. Nick waved them over. Both men were sweating profusely when they joined Nick and gladly accepted the water.

Nick asked, "How are the dogs coming along?"

Knowing Zach rarely spoke, Josh answered, "They're doing great. Zach's been working 'Shack' sessions with all six of them." The "Shack" was a two-room, twenty-foot by twenty-foot wooden building with a variety of cabinets, shelves, and closed compartments. The building was used to train the dogs in detecting explosives, narcotics, or other substances depending on the specific skills required by the customer.

"Great," said Nick, "we've only got a week of training left if we're going to meet that delivery date."

"Don't worry," said Josh. "Zach's working his magic. They'll be ready."

"Good," said Nick. "You guys go ahead and continue with the TSA dogs today. I'll be working with Gunner and Smoky. They're both due to be delivered to Atlanta next week."

Nick saw Isaiah Robinson walking into the Academy and headed back to the office to meet him. Isaiah, affectionately referred to as "Old Man Robinson," had been a fixture around this part of Johns Island for as long as anyone could remember. Nick figured him to be close to ninety. His pitch-black, weathered face carried a perpetual smile, even though the majority of his teeth were gone. A few years back, Isaiah started hanging around the kennels to watch Nick and Josh work the dogs. He'd show up riding his bike that looked to be about half as old as he was. Nick had gotten to know Isaiah and eventually offered him a part-time job cleaning out the kennels and feeding the dogs.

Nick noticed Isaiah was breathing hard, and sweat was dripping from his forehead. "Isaiah, you all right? Where's your bike?"

"It be broke, Mr. Nick. Don't rightly know what be wrong with it. Just don't go no more. I walked today. Know them dogs needs me to feed and taked care of 'em."

Isaiah got the bike after returning from the Korean War. He hadn't done much to it with the exception of changing its tires and seat a few times.

Nick patted Isaiah on the back and said, "Isaiah, the dogs can wait. You go on inside the office and rest up a bit. Get yourself something to drink."

CHAPTER FIVE

NICK, JOSH, AND Zach continued to run the dogs through their paces, being careful not to overwork them as the temperature continued to creep up throughout the afternoon. The branches on the old oak next to the trailer seemed to hang lower than usual, their leaves motionless in the afternoon sun.

Nick also kept an eye on Isaiah, who was laboring under the intense heat and humidity. It was about 4:00 p.m. when Nick called it quits for the day. Back in the office, he grabbed a Coke for himself and a beer for Josh. Zach and Sally didn't drink alcohol and opted for a cold glass of sweet tea. Isaiah was still out in the kennels tending to the dogs.

"I saw Allen this morning at The Cup," Nick said. "He's feeling better and was anxious to get back to work." Nick looked at Josh and Zach and said, "He also told me how much he appreciated what you two did for him. He'll be out here for the cookout Sunday to thank you personally."

"I'm surprised he's back so soon considering the beating he took," Josh said. "His face looked like a used piñata."

"You're right about that." Nick passed on the information about the upcoming meeting with Stanley Scott and that both Josh and Zach needed to attend. "I don't know how long the meeting's going to last, but both of you better plan on working this weekend."

"Way ahead of you, Nick. Planned on that already," Josh said.

"Good. Oh, and also keep an eye on Isaiah. I'm a little worried about him, especially with this heat."

It was approaching 4:45 p.m. when Sally reminded Nick that he'd be meeting Amy at AC's that evening. "I remember, Sally. Next thing I know, you'll be walking me over from my apartment yourself."

Sally chuckled and shooed him away. "You go home and get yourself cleaned up. You smell like a dog!"

Nick smiled and acknowleged he could do with a shower and shave. He was still concerned with Isaiah and asked Sally to drop him off on her way home.

"Be happy to. Now you get out of here and take care of that lady of yours!"

~~~

Nick drove home, cleaned up, and walked up Cannon to King Street to meet Amy at AC's. She was already seated, and after he joined her, they ordered sandwiches and iced tea.
~~~

"How was your day?" Amy asked.

"Pretty standard, but guess whose beaten-down ass I ran into at The Cup this morning?"

"What? You mean Allen's up and around? That's great! How is he?"

"Actually, he looked pretty good considering what happened. How was your day?"

"Great, I met my administrator at school this morning. She said the principal at Daniel Island Elementary wants me to do my student teaching there."

"Congratulations! I heard that's a great school. Didn't you tell me if you do a good job, there's a decent chance they'll offer you a full-time position when you graduate?"

"That would be great. I need to start earning some real money. I think Mom is really ready for me to take over some of the bills she's been paying since I've been in school. Did you talk to Allen about Sunday?"

"Yep, he's coming and bringing his assistant, Sarah, and her husband."

As the waitress brought their sandwiches, Amy told him more about her upcoming student teaching at her new school. They finished their meal, and their plates were being cleared when Amy's phone rang. She saw the number and told Nick it was Angela. She took the call and listened intently for almost a minute before saying, "That's terrible. Did they call the police?"

Nick mouthed, "What is it?"

Amy held up her hand and continued listening. "All right," she finally said, "just take care of your mom. I'll see you tomorrow." Amy looked shaken when she disconnected the call.

"What?" Nick said.

"Angela said somebody spray-painted her mom's church in North Charleston. They used the 'N'-word' and a lot of other nasty stuff. They also threw gasoline on the front door of the church and lit it. God, Nick, the whole church could have burned down if it wasn't made of stone."

"Jesus, is her mom okay?"

"Yeah, nobody was hurt, but you can imagine how upset she is. Her mom loves that church. Angela says she's there all the time."

"Did anyone see who did it?"

"No. The police are there now....God, Nick. I can't believe stuff like this is still happening here."

Nick shook his head. "I know, but it is. Remember Mother Emanuel and Charlottesville. I'll call Steve Williams tomorrow. He'll probably have more information about what happened."

"It just makes me sick," Amy said.

The news of the attack on Angela's mom's church left both Nick and Amy feeling numb. They decided to make it an early evening. Nick walked Amy to her car and, after a quick kiss goodnight, headed home. When he got back to his condo, he walked down to the end of the hall and knocked on Allen's door.

Allen opened the door. "Hey, Nick." Seeing the solemn look on Nick's face, he said, "What's wrong?"

Nick walked into the condo and said, "Did you hear what happened at the Union Baptist Church in North Charleston?"

"Yeah, I was just watching it on the news," Allen said. "They said this was the second attack on a black church in the last month."

"That's the church Angela's mom goes to. Amy and I were at AC's when Angela called and told us what happened. She's pretty upset."

"I can imagine," Allen said. "Seems like more of this kind of stuff is happening. We had a few guys at Homeland who concentrated on keeping tabs on alt-right and white nationalist groups."

"What did they do?"

"Mostly hack into their websites and work with the FBI to keep track of what they were up to. Terrorist groups like ISIS, Al-Qaeda, and Boko Haram get most of the headlines nowadays, but homegrown terrorists are probably more of a threat here in the States. The FBI has worked hard over the years to infiltrate many of these domestic groups."

"Do you think the FBI will get involved with what happened today?"

"I'm sure, but don't know how much," Allen said. "If no one was hurt, I imagine they'll probably leave most of it to the local police. It'd be nice to tell Angela what the cops are doing about this. Why don't you call your old boss?"

"Yeah, I planned on calling Steve tomorrow."

"I suppose I can check with my contacts in Washington and see what's up," Allen said.

"Good. It'd be nice to know what's going on, especially with this stuff happening so close to home."

"Right. I'll let you know what I find out." Allen said.

CHAPTER SIX

ALLEN AND ANGELA were already at The Cup when Nick arrived early Thursday morning. He gave Angela a sympathetic hug before sitting down. "How's your mom holding up?"

"Zach and I were with her last night. She's doing better, but that church is a big part of her life and it hit her hard."

"I know," Nick said. "I'm going to see what I can find out from a friend on the force."

"Thanks. Allen was telling me he's going to call someone he worked with in Washington. I can't understand how someone could do something so hateful."

"Yeah," Nick said, "seems like more of this stuff's happening. I heard another black church was vandalized this month. Anyway, I'll let you know what I find out."

"Thanks, I appreciate that."

"Well," Allen said, "on a lighter note, what time do you want us out at the Academy on Sunday?"

"Around one o'clock or so," Nick said. Turning toward Angela, he added, "Do you think your mom would like to come?"

"That's nice of you, Nick, but I'm sure she'll be at the church most of the day."

"Okay, but tell her she's welcome. I've gotta run," Nick said. "Allen, see you out at the airport at 11:30."

"Right," answered Allen.

Nick left The Cup and phoned Steve Williams on his way to Johns Island. He explained that his friend's mom was a member of the church that was defaced and asked if he had any more information that wasn't in last night's news.

"Don't know all the specifics," Steve said, "but I can tell you we've been noticing an uptick in Internet activity by several white supremacist groups, specifically from a particular Klan spinoff. They call themselves the Confederate White Knights. Something's definitely in the wind."

"Interesting," Nick said. "Do you have any idea what may be coming?"

"Look, Nick, we got history, and I don't mind helping you out where I can. But you need to let us deal with this. I got my ass chewed out when you and your guys got involved in the DiMarco thing."

"I understand, Steve. Just let me know what you can about the church attack. That's my friend Angela's mom's church."

Nick disconnected the call as he was pulling into the Academy. Josh and Zach were already in the field working the dogs. Sally was at her desk when Nick walked in the office.

"Zach told me what happened to the church where Angela's mom goes. Just terrible. Breaks my heart. I put a few messages on your desk," she said.

Nick checked his messages and then joined Josh and Zach outside for the next few hours until the three of them left for the meeting with Stanley Scott.

When they arrived at the Hilton, Scott led the group into the meeting room and introduced his assistant, Jennifer White, who had been chatting with Allen. After everyone was seated, Scott removed a tape recorder from his briefcase. "Jennifer will be taking notes, and I'll be recording our discussion today. I assume that's acceptable."

"No problem here," Nick said, gesturing to Josh and Zach, who nodded their approval.

"Good," Mr. Scott said. "Before we get started, let me explain what you can expect over the next few weeks and months. Mr. Miller and Mr. Giordano will be receiving subpoenas to appear for a deposition. I'm not sure the exact date, but I've spoken to Mr. Rossini's attorney, Phillip Bryson, and he's agreed to schedule your depositions on the same day here in Charleston. You'll both be served this morning here at the Hilton. So, that should be happening sometime during our meeting. You'll also be receiving interrogatories, which Jennifer and I will help you answer."

He continued, "Now, Allen, what documents do you have relating to information you uncovered about the theft of drugs and the syndicate's activities out at the Westcott company?"

Allen thought for a moment before answering. "The only hard copy relating to the theft at Mercy was created by my assistant, Sarah Pryor. It's a general description of how we discovered who was behind the theft. She prepared it for Charleston's chief of police. As far as Westcott goes, most all of what I discovered is on my computers."

"Okay," Scott said. "I would expect Mr. Bryson to issue a subpoena duces tecum requiring you to produce whatever documents you have and perhaps your computers themselves. Jennifer and I will prep both of you before the actual depositions. Mr. Bryson told me he would like to schedule the depositions as soon as possible. He mentioned a date in early to mid-November. That'll be tight, but we should have time to answer his interrogatories and produce any documents requested.

"I expect we'll need a good day to prepare for your depositions. There's nothing for either of you to worry about. Just answer whatever questions you're asked honestly and succinctly. Don't volunteer information not germane to the question. We'll know the actual date when you're served today. Then we can schedule a date to prep you. Any questions?"

"No," answered Nick, "I've been through this process a number of times."

"Same here," Allen added. "I participated in a few of those during my time in Washington."

"Good," Scott said. But before he could continue, there was a knock on the door. An individual entered and asked if Mr. Nicholas Giordano and Mr. Allen Miller were present.

Nick and Allen acknowleged his question. The man then served the subpoenas and quickly left the room.

"Let me take a look at those," Scott said. "Okay, they're both scheduled for Wednesday, November 15, at the U.S. Attorney's Office here in Charleston. Let's plan on Jennifer and me coming back Monday the thirteenth. That'll give us plenty of time to prepare. Will that work for you?"

"Fine with me," Nick said.

"No problem here," added Allen.

"Good."

Scott pressed the record button and began the interview, first noting the date and location and then identifying himself, Miss White, Nick, Josh, and Zach. "Let me give you some background before we get into the specifics of what happened here in Charleston. A group of us at the U.S. Attorney's Office in New Jersey have been working closely with the Justice Department in Washington to develop a case against several individuals associated with the Genovese crime family—the largest of the five organized crime families in New York and New Jersey. In 2016, Liborio "Barney" Bellomo became the boss of the Genovese family, and our ultimate goal is to indict Bellomo on RICO charges.

"We're building our case against Bellomo, but he's so well insulated by the organization it's difficult to link him directly to specific racketeering crimes. We now believe our best shot of getting to Bellomo is by convicting Mario Rossini—one of his main underbosses. The grand jury has already indicted Rossini, and he'll stand trial in about four months.

"We were excited when Max DiMarco agreed to testify against Mr. Rossini. But, as you know, DiMarco was assassinated in prison. His associate, Mr. Angelo Vitale, is also in prison in South Carolina, but we don't believe he can connect Rossini to any specific criminal activity carried out here in Charleston."

Scott turned to Allen. "I'd like you to walk us through how you first got involved in all this, as well as the subsequent events that led to the arrests of DiMarco and Vitale. You other gentlemen can add your observations as Allen takes us through what happened."

"All right," Allen said. "I'll do my best. The whole thing started back in July when I met with Mr. Jack Rennells, the CEO of MediGroup out of Chicago. The company owns a good number of hospitals in the Midwest and South—including Mercy General in Charleston. Rennells got a call from his VP at Mercy who believed narcotics, mainly oxycodone and other pain pills, were being stolen from the hospital."

"Excuse me, Mr. Miller," Jennifer interrupted. "What's the name of the VP you just mentioned?"

"Sorry. His name is Charles Summerton. Mr. Rennells asked me to investigate. He impressed on me that the investigation needed to be done in secret. Apparently, MediGroup was in discussions to acquire another hospital, and any scandal would kill those negotiations. In addition, if he brought the police in, whoever was behind the theft would know about it. He wanted me to covertly access Mercy's computer system and try to figure out if drugs were being taken and, if so, who was involved."

Mr. Scott interrupted. "Excuse me. Did you sign any sort of non-disclosure agreement with MediGroup or Mercy Hospital?"

"Yes, I did. The letter of confidentiality I signed covered both MediGroup and Mercy."

Scott made a note and said, "Thank you. Please continue."

"It took several weeks, but my assistant, Sarah Pryor, and I finally discovered that the drugs were being stolen when they were delivered to the hospital's shipping department. I downloaded digital files from several security cameras in the department. That's when we discovered that two employees, named Logan Jefferies and Scott Evans, were responsible for the thefts. I have to admit, the way these guys stole the drugs was amazingly clever. The bulk of the hospital's narcotics was delivered every Friday afternoon by a local distributor."

"What was the name of the company supplying the narcotics?" Ms. White asked.

"Franklin Pharmaceuticals. They have a warehouse in Summerville. Anyway, the drugs were delivered in sealed bins and taken to a separate room in the shipping department. That's where the two workers I mentioned checked the shipment against the paperwork. We later discovered they were working with a guy named Jerry Shields, the manager of Mercy's cybersecurity department."

Allen described how he and his assistant discovered the clever way DiMarco was hijacking narcotics through a system of modified POs and manipulated security footage.

"At that point, we knew when the narcotics were being stolen but couldn't understand how they got them out of the hospital. Sarah finally figured it out. The way they got the stuff out was surprisingly simple.

"She noticed the vending machine in the room was serviced every Friday afternoon. A man from the vending company would restock the soft drinks, unlock and remove the money container, and replace it with a new one. Then he'd use a separate key to unlock and remove another container from the side of the machine. This seemed strange to us. Why the second container? Sarah contacted several vending machine manufacturers, and none of their machines had a second side container. It became obvious the drugs were being put in that container during the gap in the security footage. All the vending guy had to do was remove the side container with the drugs and slide a new one in. Amazingly simple, and who's going to check some vending guy?

"Now we believed we knew both when and how the drugs were stolen, but we needed a recording that showed the drugs actually being taken and transferred to the machine.

"Here's where it may get a little confusing, so stay with me. While all this was going on, I discovered there'd been an unusual amount of turnover in the shipping department, and Chuck Thompson—he was the manager of that department— had abruptly resigned. A few months before that, Mr. Chris Davis, the purchasing manager, became seriously ill and took a leave of absence. Both of these guys were in their early forties and longtime employees at Mercy. These three things raised a red flag. I researched Thompson and Davis, using both internal files and external data. The results shed more light on what was happening at Mercy.

"First, I hacked into Davis's medical records, and they showed symptoms of acute kidney disease. I also found a kidney biopsy that showed the presence of oxalate crystals, a clear indication he'd been exposed to ethylene glycol, the key ingredient in antifreeze and deicing agents. As crazy as it sounded, he must have ingested it in some form or another.

"Next, I looked into Thompson, and the results were surprising. Thompson's bank records showed only minimal balances in both his personal checking and savings accounts. I discovered there had been a series of $7,500 withdrawals from his savings account over the previous ten months. These withdrawals ended the month he resigned from the hospital.

"I hacked into his computer's web browser and discovered he made multiple visits to an Internet betting site. It became clear that Chuck Thompson had a serious gambling problem. The $7,500 monthly withdrawals turned out to be payments to a loan sharking operation run by a man named Anthony Grasso. This Grasso guy was a major player in the Charleston mob. There now seemed to be a clear connection between the drug thefts at Mercy and a much larger criminal operation.

"Whatever doubt we had disappeared when someone slit Thompson's throat in the Citadel Mall parking lot."

"Excuse me," Mr. Scott said, "you said you had permission from both Mr. Rennells and Mr. Summerton to access information from Mercy's computers, correct?"

"Right," Allen replied.

"However, any information you obtained from Mr. Thompson's personal bank records will not be admissible in court. Bryson will definitely use this to discredit your testimony. But we'll deal with that later. Please go ahead."

"Okay. This is pretty much where Nick got involved. We knew the guy servicing the hospital vending machine must be part of it. So, we waited for him to make his regular Friday pickup and then followed him to a warehouse in North Charleston. The name of the place was Westcott Distributing. When I got into Westcott's computers, it became clear the company was a front for a series of smaller cash businesses. Whoever owned Westcott was laundering money. But I still didn't have actual proof of any of this. I was creating a paper trail I hoped would lead to who owned Westcott, but I ran out of time before I could finish."

"Anything from Westcott computers will also be inadmissible during trial," Scott said. "We may be able to get around that problem, but we'll worry about that later. Please go ahead. What happened next."

Allen continued, "The next day, a Sunday, I accessed Mercy's purchasing department's computer and sent Franklin Pharmaceuticals a bogus order for drugs that needed to be delivered the next day. As soon as I sent it, I deleted it from purchasing's computers, created a fake PO, and got it delivered to Logan Jefferies. Remember, he was one of the two guys that were taking the drugs.

"The computer guy, Shields, didn't know anything about the shipment and wouldn't be watching the security cameras to freeze the footage. All we had to do was record Jefferies and Evans stealing the drugs and putting them in the vending machine. If it worked, we'd have the solid evidence we needed to take to the authorities.

"As crazy as it sounds, the thing actually worked. I got a recording of Jefferies and Evans stealing the drugs and putting them into that side container in the vending machine! I told Mr. Rennells what we had, and we arranged to get the evidence to the Charleston police that evening. But Sarah and I never made it to the police department. That's when I got knocked out and drugged by Vitale and Grasso. Luckily, Sarah saw them putting me in the back of a black van and called Nick." Allen turned to Nick and said, "That's pretty much all I remember until I woke up in the hospital. Nick's going to have to take it from here."

"Okay," Nick began, "Josh, Zach, and I were out at the Academy—my police dog training business on Johns Island—when I got Sarah's call. She was frantic but managed to tell me what happened to Allen. When she mentioned the black van, I knew exactly where they were taking him. Allen and I'd seen a black van out at Westcott when we followed the vending truck to the warehouse. I knew what Allen was in for once those guys got him to that warehouse.

"Josh and Zach didn't know anything about what was going on, but I knew I'd need their help. Josh had his Beretta locked in his truck. I gave Zach my 12-gauge, and I grabbed my bolt-action Browning. I was going to call my friend Steve

Williams—he was my boss when I was a K-9 officer in North Charleston—but got sidetracked when Josh put Ringo in the truck. Ringo's one of our German Shepherds. Anyway, we took off for the warehouse, and I gave my guys the short version of what had happened and what we'd probably be up against. They didn't even bat an eye. We were almost at the Westcott place when I realized I hadn't called Steve. I got ahold of him, and he said he'd get officers to the warehouse as soon as possible.

"When we got there, I saw the black van along with DiMarco and Vitale's cars parked outside the building. Josh reconned the place. They had Allen tied up inside—Josh said he was already messed up pretty bad. I figured we couldn't wait for the police, so we took up positions around the warehouse. That's when all hell broke loose. Josh took out one of DiMarco's guys, and Zach blew away Grasso with the shotgun. Vitale tried to run for it, but Ringo took him down and chewed him up pretty good. DiMarco made it out of the warehouse and was almost in his car when I got to him. He pulled a gun, and I shot him in the shoulder. The whole thing felt like a Quentin Tarantino movie—a real bloodbath."

"Excuse me," Scott said, "when one of DiMarco's men was shot, who initiated the gunfire?"

"I was the first to fire when I took a shot at the van. We didn't have any choice."

"I understand completely," Scott replied, "but there's no doubt Mr. Bryson will argue that DiMarco and his men were acting in self-defense."

"That's nuts!" Josh said. "There's no way Allen would have made it out alive if we hadn't done what we did."

Scott quickly answered, "I understand. All I'm saying is that's the argument you can expect from their lawyer. Mr. Giordano, please continue with what happened next."

"Okay. A few minutes later, Steve and three squad cars showed up. Grasso and another guy were dead, and the cops took DiMarco and Vitale into custody. The EMTs patched them up, and two police officers took them away for processing. Allen was in bad shape when the EMTs got to him. They were able to get him stabilized and transported to the hospital. We spent another two hours being interrogated by two North Charleston detectives. They finally let us go around 9:00 p.m. that night. I know I probably left out a bunch of details, but that's basically what happened after Allen was kidnapped."

"Thank you," Scott said. "You both did a good job giving us an idea what went on and who was involved. Your testimony could be helpful to our case. I'm amazed at what you were able to accomplish. Very impressive.

"As I said before, our primary goal is to develop an air-tight case against Mr. Rossini. One impediment to that is Bryson, Rossini's lawyer. Bryson's an extremely competent attorney and has been very effective in protecting Rossini over the years. He graduated first in his class at Harvard Law and spent ten years at the U.S. Attorney's Office in New York City before jumping ship to represent Rossini. We're hoping that the company DiMarco used to launder money for the Rossini syndicate could be the link we need to finally nail him. That's where we need your additional cooperation.

"Allen, if the paper trail you started to put together can be connected to Rossini's mob, we may have enough to get him. How far did you actually get in finding out who really owns Westcott?"

"I did find several shell companies and offshore banks that were used to muddy the waters," Allen answered. "But I was kidnapped before I could get into it much further and haven't done anything with it since I got out of the hospital."

"I understand," Scott said. "We have some very capable cyber professionals at the Justice Department. We'll subpoena Westcott's records, and they'll follow up on that."

"I'd be happy to work with them," Allen offered.

"I appreciate that, but this is the same situation when you hacked into Mr. Thompson's personal computer. The fact that you illegally accessed Westcott's computer system means none of what you learned can be used in court. We'll need to do this legally. Furthermore, I'm sure you're aware that you could potentially be hit with a class B misdemeanor or felony for hacking. We'll have a judge issue a warrant for Westcott's computers, and our people will take it from there."

Allen understood the criminal laws on hacking as well as anyone. "Yep, that makes a lot of sense."

Mr. Scott smiled and said, "But you will need to respond to any questions about what you did if asked in your deposition. Mr. Bryson knows perfectly well any information you uncovered from Thompson and Westcott's computers is inadmissible. I doubt he'll want to pursue any charges against you. If he did, he runs the risk of bringing to light what you did learn.

"Again, our problem is that we don't know how much of this information the court will allow us to use. As I said, Mr. Bryson will argue that everything you obtained from computers external to Mercy will be inadmissible. And I have no doubt the judge will agree with him. We can also expect him to attempt to exclude information obtained from Mercy's computers. Here we're in a much stronger position. Recent litigation has confirmed the right of an employer to monitor and access employee information as long as it's done on company computers.

"But now to another matter. The work Allen and the rest of you did struck a major blow to the syndicate's operations in Charleston. And we know those operations were connected to Rossini's organization in New Jersey. We also know the mob will attempt to reestablish its narcotics business here. I think it's safe to say these people know a good deal about each of you. It's obvious Allen and Mrs. Pryor pose the greatest danger to the mob, but each of you played a part in what happened."

Sidney Scott let that sink in before he continued. "Of course, we don't know how much the Jersey syndicate knows about you people. But they'll certainly want to find out whether any of you can connect what Westcott was doing with Rossini."

"So," Allen said, "what you're basically saying is that these mob guys would feel much better if we all somehow disappeared. Right?"

"Listen," Scott replied, "these criminal organizations usually don't run around killing people like in the movies. They have their lawyers to do their dirty work. I just want you to be aware of the situation and be careful. As a practical matter, there are a few obvious things to consider. Keep your doors locked. Try not to be out late at night alone. Change your daily routine. And if anything seems threatening or out of the ordinary, contact the police. I know Mr. Giordano was a police officer, and Mr. Taylor and Mr. Brown served in the Army. You've all been in dangerous situations, and I'm sure you'll act accordingly."

Scott nodded toward Allen and said, "And Mr. Miller, your experience at US-CERT and your security clearance leads me to believe you can handle yourself." It was clear that Sidney Scott had done his homework on Allen and his friends.

"I think all of us understand what you're saying," Nick said. "But my concern is with other people who may not have had direct involvement but still might be exposed. People like my secretary, Allen's assistant, and my girlfriend."

"Yes, Allen's secretary, Mrs. Pryor, should be made aware of the situation, as she was certainly involved," Scott said. "However, Mr. Taylor, Mr. Brown, and the other individuals you mentioned are probably not viewed as a threat and should be safe. Finally, the best advice I can give you is stay away from anything that has to do with Westcott. Let us handle it from now on."

Allen and Nick had a few more questions for Scott, and when they were finished, Scott said, "Jennifer and I'll be back here before your deposition. But in the meantime, please feel free to contact either one of us if you have any questions or concerns."

The meeting was about to break up when Josh spoke up. "I've got a question."

"Certainly," Scott said.

"As far as I can see, you people have plenty of stuff that connects what happened here with those guys in New Jersey. There's those tapes Allen made, and you said your computer people should be able to trace Westcott back to the syndicate in New Jersey."

"You're right about all that," Scott said, "but in the courts, the burden of proof lies with us as the prosecution, and it's not what you know—it's only what you can prove. But assuming we can prove Westcott's owned by the Jersey syndicate, we've got a decent case. But again, we'll be up against Rossini's lawyer, and Phillip Bryson is as good as they come."

"Yeah, but you just said we might not be a threat to the syndicate. Right? But now you want Nick and Allen to testify. How's that not a threat to them?"

"I understand what you're saying," Scott replied, "and we're going to do everything in our power to keep all of you safe. It all hinges on Mr. Bryson's ability to convince the judge to rule that the information we have is inadmissible. This trial will be our best chance to begin to dismantle one of the most powerful and destructive criminal organizations in the country. Your cooperation is key in making that happen."

Scott and White expressed their appreciation, and the meeting broke up. As Nick and his friends headed to the parking lot, it was clear that Josh was less than thrilled with what he'd heard.

"Well," Josh said, "that didn't make me feel all warm and fuzzy."

"Yeah," Nick added. "I was hoping that with DiMarco and his cronies out of the picture, we could put this whole thing behind us. I guess that was wishful thinking. I'll make sure Amy, Sally, and Isaiah know what's happened. Allen, go ahead and tell Angela and Sarah. They need to know what's going on."

"I agree," Allen said, "but at least now we know where we stand. And Scott was right—we all need to watch our backs until this thing blows over."

CHAPTER SEVEN

THE HEATWAVE WAS short-lived, and by Sunday morning, pleasant weather had once again returned to the Lowcountry. The skies were crystal clear, and the temperature had settled in the low seventies by the time everyone arrived at the Academy for the cookout.

Nick had just tapped the small keg of beer he'd picked up at Low Tide Brewery the day before. Sally, Amy, and Angela were preparing the food. The hot dogs and burgers were complemented by Caesar salad and fried okra. Josh was giving Sarah and her husband, Dave, a quick tour of the grounds, while Pink Floyd, the Stones, and Fleetwood Mac played over the speakers Nick had mounted outside the office.

Nick and Allen were seated together enjoying the weather when Nick asked, "Hey Allen, any luck finding more information about the church thing?"

"Yeah, got ahold of one of my friends in Washington and told her what happened at Union Baptist. She knew about it and the other church attack."

"Are they doing anything about it?"

"Well, yes and no," Allen said. "The problem is the number of these hate groups has skyrocketed over the last few years. There are over a thousand now operating inside the U.S.—ten years ago it was closer to a hundred! The KKK, Neo-Nazis, and white nationalist groups have been around for a long time. But the alt-right and all the anti-Muslim racially charged rhetoric have produced an explosion of these organizations on an unprecedented scale. And several of these groups have a predisposition toward violence and have increased their paramilitary capabilities. My friends at CERT are doing their best, but my contact told me it's tough to stay on top of it with all the other international terrorist activity."

"I know that, but are they going to do anything about the attacks?" Nick repeated.

"That's the 'yes and no' part. Homeland Security will continue to monitor, but the local FBI field office in Charleston will be dealing directly with it. And the local police will obviously be involved, too. She didn't have any more information, but she'll let me know if anything else pops up on their radar. How about you? Any luck with your guy?"

After Nick relayed Steve's information on the Confederate White Knights, Allen replied, "That's good to know, but I wish we had something more we could tell Angela."

"Couldn't you help us out with a little hacking?" Nick asked. "Just take a quick peek to see if they had anything to do with what happen at the church? You're the computer whiz. You could hack the website for these people, right?"

"Yeah, I could. But remember what happened the last time I did that. Plus, we don't even know if these White Knight people were the group behind the attacks."

"I know," Nick said. "I'm just saying couldn't you just take a quick peek to see if they had anything to do with what happen at the church?"

Allen laughed. "A quick peek? That's all you want me to do?"

Nick smiled. "Yeah, just a little peek. Seriously, Allen, you know how shook up Angela and her mom were. And I'm not sure I'm going to get much more from Steve. He's still pissed about Westcott."

Allen shook his head and finally said, "All right, I'll think about it."

"Great," Nick said. "Now, let's go cook some hamburgers!"

The food was great, and everyone enjoyed a lazy afternoon as warm southern breezes graced the Lowcountry. Zach finally convinced Isaiah to share some of his old Gullah stories. Isaiah obliged, took center stage, and began spinning his yarns.

The party started to wind down around 6:30 p.m., with everyone pitching in to help clean up. Nick told Josh and Zach he'd stick around to make sure the dogs were settled. Allen had driven Sarah and Dave, and they were the first to leave. Sally was nice enough to drop Isaiah off on her way home, and Josh,

Zach, and Angela decided to stop by the Crazy Owl before Angela headed back to North Charleston.

Nick had just finished with the dogs and was walking back to the office with Amy. She slipped her arm through his and said, "What a fun afternoon. I really enjoyed finally meeting Sarah and her husband."

"Yeah," Nick said. "Sarah seemed really sharp, and Dave's a nice guy."

"Speaking of nice guys, are we still set to see your dad next weekend?"

"Definitely. I've been thinking about him more lately. With the business and everything, I haven't got up to the farm as much as I should. He's still in good shape, but he's going to be 68 in January." Nick smiled, his eyes going to the middle distance. "You know, when you're a kid, your dad seems bigger than life. In your eyes as a child, he's the smartest, strongest, and bravest person you know. But the older you get, the more you can see his faults and flaws. But at the same time, you grow to appreciate him even more. I guess in the end that's what it's all about."

"That's sweet, Nick." Amy gave him one of her sly smiles. "I still say we should get your dad and my mom together. You never know."

Nick laughed. "That would be a little weird. And when did you become a matchmaker?"

Amy pulled Nick closer and whispered, "Well, I always thought we'd be a good match, so I've got a hundred percent success rate so far."

Nick smiled. "Can't argue with that."

The sun tumbled over the trees toward the horizon, and the sky was awash with a warm red-orange glow, a scattering of clouds catching the final scarlet rays. It was the time of day when you can feel the quiet settling softly, the day yielding to night. The outdoor lights on the office trailer had just come on, and Nick and Amy sat at the picnic table enjoying the moment.

Amy took Nick's hand and said, "I love this time of the day. Everything slows down and relaxes."

"I know," Nick said. "Sometimes when I'm out here by myself on evenings like this, I'll take out one of the dogs. We just sit and take it all in. I think they enjoy it as much as we do."

"How long have the dogs been keeping these romantic sunsets with Nick Giordano to themselves?" Amy asked playfully.

"Since Max, I suppose," Nick said softly. "He was the only dog I had on the force. We took in a lot of sunsets together."

Amy remembered seeing a picture of Nick in his dress uniform, his dog at his side, and she immediately regretted her teasing. She knew that Nick was still suffering from the trauma of the shootout that had claimed the lives of Max and Billy Freeman, Nick's fellow officer. "I'm sorry, Nick. I shouldn't have said that."

"No, not at all. I had four great years with Max. I'm not saying I'll ever completely get over what happened to Billy, but as time passes, you tend to remember the good times and bury the bad. I guess I put all that in a place I don't visit very often but will never forget."

Amy smiled. "Well, I'm glad you have these dogs. I know how much they mean to you."

"Yeah, they're pretty neat," Nick said. "You know, dogs were the first animals to be domesticated back during the last ice age about fifteen thousand years ago. At least that's what the anthropologists say. What's really interesting is that dogs' ancestors are wolves. So, you've got to figure that at some point their ancestors and our ancestors were enemies. But you can imagine how those hunter-gatherers must have eventually realized how valuable these wolf-dogs could be for protection and hunting. Together they must have made a pretty awesome combination." Nick laughed. "Well, that's my little anthropology lecture for today."

Amy batted her eyes and said, "Very enlightening, professor. I've got an idea. Let's go back to my place, and I'll give you an anatomy lesson."

"I'm good with that," Nick said with a smile. "You know how I love to learn things."

Nick locked up, and they walked to his truck arm in arm—with Nick thinking just how lucky he was to have found Amy. Twenty-five minutes later, he pulled into a parking spot in front of Amy's James Island apartment. They hurried inside, neither noticing the light-brown Ford Taurus that had followed them or the large man seated behind the wheel taking pictures.

Carlo Tucci waited patiently outside Amy's appartment for the next two hours until Nick finally left at 9:30 p.m. and drove back to his apartment. After parking his truck in the building's underground garage, Nick took the elevator up to his sixth-floor apartment. Once satisfied that Nick was in his apartment, Tucci drove back to his hotel.

~~~

Earlier that evening, Allen returned to his condo after dropping off Sarah and Dave. He'd been thinking about Nick's suggestion to check out that racist group. After making a pot of coffee, he logged into his Mac Pro and began researching the Confederate White Knights and some of the other white nationalist groups active in South Carolina.

The original White Knights were considered the most militant and violent chapter of the Ku Klux Klan. They were formed in Mississippi in the early 1960s. Within a year, their membership had soared to over four thousand, and they were responsible for a series of bombings, church burnings, beatings, and murders.

In 1964, a wave of northern civil rights activists traveled to several southern states in what was called Freedom Summer. Their main goal was to promote racial equality and bring more black people to the polls by convincing them to register to vote. Three of these activists, students from Ohio, were stopped while driving through Mississippi by the Neshoba County sheriff, who just happened to be a member of the KKK. The three were arrested and jailed while members of the White Knights worked out the details of their murder. Less than an hour after their release, the activists were killed and
~~~

buried at a construction site near a dam. A bulldozer was used to cover their bodies with tons of dirt.

The murders were investigated, but only two of the twelve White Knights involved in the killings were indicted and convicted. These gruesome murders received national attention, and the local chapter of the White Knights was soon disbanded. But other chapters remained active, including the one formed in South Carolina.

As time passed, social norms evolved and new federal and state laws put pressure on many of these hate groups. But in the last few years, that trend had reversed itself, with radical groups once again on the rise. The Aryan Nation, Neo-Nazis, anti-Muslim, and other white separatist groups made headlines recently with tragedies like the Mother Emanuel Church shooting in Charleston and the violent "Unite the Right" rally in Charlottesville.

Allen also discovered that while some of these groups are vocal in their bigotry, some are not. The Confederate White Knights fall into the latter category. That they seemed to be more active lately was both surprising and unsettling. Allen could find very little on the South Carolina branch, but he relished a challenge and the secretive nature of this group only hardened his resolve to find out more.

CHAPTER EIGHT

THE FOLLOWIN MORNING, Carlo Tucci was up early, continuing his efforts to identify and familiarize himself with his targets and their routines. Carlo took his time in matters such as these. He never rushed things—doing so was often a one-way ticket to your own funeral. Based on what he'd learned from Petrelli, Miller and Giordano often met in the morning at a coffeehouse close to the building where they both lived. Carlo arrived at The Coffee Cup at approximately 6:30 a.m., bought a coffee and newspaper, and settled in.

He was surprised to see the same woman he'd watched at the apartment the night before working behind the counter. He made a mental note to learn more about her. Forty minutes later, Nick entered the shop. After a short conversation with the woman behind the counter, he picked up a coffee and muffin and took a seat a few tables away from where he was seated.

A short time later, another man and a black girl dressed in hospital scrubs arrived. After getting coffee, they joined the first man. Carlo knew the two men were Allen Miller, the computer guy, and Nick Giordano, the dog trainer.

Carlo folded the paper, placed it on the table, and removed what appeared to be an iPhone and earbuds. In reality, the phone was a reconnaissance device capable of taking high-definition pictures and recording conversations up to one hundred feet from the source. He then laid the device on top of his paper, positioning it so that it bypassed the kaleidoscope of conversations and found a direct line of sight to the table where Nick, Allen, and Angela were seated. He listened.

"Thanks for yesterday," Angela said. "What a fun day."

"Yeah," Allen added. "Sarah and Dave really enjoyed meeting the whole crew."

"Thanks guys," Nick said. "We'll definitely do that more often."

Angela pulled out her phone and began sharing some of the pictures she'd taken the day before at the cookout. Nick was scrolling through her shots when he noticed a photo of Zach standing with his arm around an older gray-haired woman.

"Angela, is that your mom?" Nick asked.

"Yeah, I took that the other night. Zach came over for dinner. Mama loves the guy. And would you believe it, he actually carries on conversations with her?"

"That's amazing." Nick chuckled and said, "The best Josh and I can get out of him is an occasional grunt. And look at him here—he's actually smiling! Wonders will never cease."

At that point, Allen got Nick's attention and nodded toward Angela. "Go ahead an tell her about the lawyer."

Nick and Allen were quiet until Angela's smile disappeared. "Uh, what? You guys look worried."

Nick watched Angela's face tighten in angry resignation as he filled her in on the attorney's warning.

"Jesus Christ," Angela sighed. "First, I gotta worry about some dumbass crackers running around attacking our churches. Now you're telling me I gotta watch out for some asshole wiseguy mob thugs from New Jersey. What the hell!"

Nick knew that when Angela got like this, there wasn't much you could do to calm her down. Allen jumped in and changed the subject by bringing everyone up to speed on what he had learned from his research the previous night. Nick added what Steve had told him about the Confederate White Knights.

Angela shook her head and said, "Christ, you'd think all those old white racist sons-of-bitches would have died off by now."

"I know," Allen said, "but it seems like they keep making new ones."

Nick checked his phone and said, "I've got to get to work. Listen, Angela, we'll keep you posted on what we find out. In the meantime, stay close to Zach."

"Come on, Angela," Allen said. "I'll walk you to the hospital."

They all got up and left The Cup, unaware that their entire conversation had been recorded. Carlo Tucci remained seated, digesting all he'd heard. There were two new players now—the nurse, Angela, and another woman named Sarah. It was clear this Sarah was in some way associated with Allen Miller. It also sounded like the nurse knew details of DiMarco's hospital scheme and his front company, Westcott Distributing. From what he'd just heard, both might have to be dealt with if Rossini ordered the situation sanitized.

When he was sure he wouldn't be noticed, he left the coffee shop and walked across Courtenay to his rented Ford Taurus. He watched Nick's Toyota pull out of the condo's garage and followed him out to the Academy. Carlo parked his car under a large oak tree about a hundred yards from the entrance to the Academy and waited.

A few minutes later, he attached a zoom lens to his camera and eased his car toward the kennel grounds, stopping for about thirty seconds while he snapped off about fifty shots of Josh and Zach working the dogs.

He drove back to the hotel and reviewed his photos—those he'd taken that day and the night before. While he studied the shots, the genesis of a plan was beginning to take shape.

CHAPTER NINE

AFTER A MORNING training the dogs, Nick, Josh, and Zach were back in the office having lunch. Sally had prepared hotdogs and salad, leftovers from Sunday's cookout. They'd just finished when Zach received a call from Angela. She told him they'd be going to Union Baptist after he picked her up from work. The police had finished their forensic work at the church, and a handful of members were meeting that evening to remove the offensive graffiti that had been spray-painted and repair the fire-damaged door.

They worked the dogs hard that afternoon, finishing around 4:30 p.m. Zach left shortly after to pick up Angela at the hospital and then swung by her house to collect her mom. It was about 6:00 p.m. by the time they all arrived at Union Baptist. Reverend Walker and a half dozen parishioners were already at work painting over the offensive words. Zach joined a few men working to repair and repaint the church's fire-damaged front door.

A small but well-maintained church, Union Baptist supported a congregation of almost 150 devoted worshipers. The Union Heights neighborhood where Angela grew up had experienced some gentrification in recent years, but it still remained one of North Charleston's roughest areas. Drugs and gang activities were still prevalent, and it wasn't uncommon to see groups of men passing a bottle around in front of one of the many liquor stores. The neighborhood still had its share of run-down storefronts and scruffy, dilapidated homes. Despite these problems, there was a strong sense of community. The church was more than 150 years old, its white stone siding and arching spire symbols of peace and tranquility in a still turbulent neighborhood. Even though Angela and her mom had moved out of Union Heights several years ago, the church remained a central part of their lives.

It was approaching 9:00 p.m. by the time the work was finally completed, and everyone was inside relaxing before heading home. Reverend Walker was leading the group in prayer. His voice was the kind that echoed both solace and hope.

The quiet moment of reflection was suddenly and violently disrupted when several of the church's stained-glass windows exploded in a hail of gunfire. Shards of glass flew as bullets riddled the wooden chancel and altar. Zach pushed Angela to the floor under one of the pews and ran toward the front door. He opened it just in time to see the dented rear end of an older red Chevy Silverado fishtail around the corner onto Piggly Wiggly Drive, burning rubber toward the I-26 ramp. It disappeared before he could get its license plate number.

Zach tore back inside, where he found Angela still lying under the pew. She was unhurt. He quickly surveyed the scene to see if anyone had been hit. There was an eerie quiet. Then Angela's scream pierced the silence. "Oh God! Mom!" Cornelia Martin was sprawled on the floor in front of the altar. She'd been shot in the chest.

Angela ran to her. Zach was right behind, his phone out dialing 911. Cornelia was conscious but bleeding profusely. Zach tore off his shirt and used it to absorb the blood and apply pressure to the wound. He knew that more than 90 percent of deaths from gunshot wounds were due to hypovolemic shock caused by a severe loss of blood.

Reverend Walker got towels and the church's medical kit and helped Zach get the bleeding under control. Zach was concerned Cornelia might go into shock before the EMTs made it to the church. Thankfully, no one else had been injured in the shooting. North Charleston police and EMTs both showed up within five minutes. The EMTs stabilized Cornelia and transported her to MUSC's Trauma Unit. Angela was by her side in the back of the van as it raced to the hospital.

Five more squad cars arrived within the next few minutes, and the crime scene was cordoned off. Once the area was secure, officers and detectives began taking statements from the remaining individuals, while the forensics team began gathering evidence. News crews from all three local stations were on the scene within twenty minutes of the shooting.

~~~
~~~

Nick was relaxing in his apartment watching Monday Night Football when the game was interrupted by the breaking news. A reporter stood in front of Union Baptist, surrounded by nine or ten police cars—their blue and red lights illuminating the front of the church.

"This is Ann Wallace from ABC News Team 4 reporting tonight from in front of the Union Baptist Church in North Charleston. At approximately nine o'clock this evening, the church was hit with a hail of gunfire from AR-15-type semiautomatic assault rifles. One person has been wounded and taken to MUSC's Trauma Unit. We know the shooting victim was a woman, but her name and condition have not been released. Union Baptist is the same church that only last week was the target of arson and spray-painted with racial slurs. It's the second church in the Charleston area to have been attacked in the past month. The North Charleston Police Department is in the process of investigating these attacks and has scheduled a press conference tomorrow morning at 10:00 a.m."

A moment later, the football game was back on the TV.

"Jesus Christ," Nick whispered to himself. He grabbed his cell and dialed Amy's number. It rang several times before going to message. He left a message telling her to call him as soon as possible and then called Zach and Angela. Neither answered. He hung up and jogged down the hall to Allen's condo.

"Come on in, Nick. What's up?"

"You haven't heard about the shooting?"

"What shooting?"

"Union Baptist Church. Someone just shot up the place, and a woman was injured. Shit Allen, Zach, Angela, and her mom were out there tonight!"

"Christ! Did they say who was shot?"

"No, just that it's a woman. I called Zach and Angela, but they didn't answer."

"Did you try Amy?"

"Yeah, no answer."

"Can't you call Lieutenant Williams?"

"If we don't find out more tonight, I'll call him first thing in the morning. I don't know what else to do. I'll keep trying Angela and Zach. Hopefully, one of them will call."

"Right," Allen said, as he turned on the TV. "Let's keep our fingers crossed."

~~~

The officers and detectives kept Zach and the other victims sequestered in the church basement while taking their individual statements. They were not permitted to use their cellphones other than to make one call to a family member.

It was almost 11:30 p.m. by the time they were cut loose. As soon as he was released, Zach called Angela. She was at the hospital and told him her mom was out of surgery and in stable condition. He drove directly to MUSC. Angela was waiting for him, and they both spent the rest of the night at the hospital.
~~~

CHAPTER TEN

NICK ROLLED INTO The Cup on Tuesday morning at 7:30 a.m. Amy saw him come in the shop and got someone to cover for her. "God, Nick, I heard on the radio what happened last night when I was driving into work," she said.

"I tried to get ahold of you last night," Nick said.

"I'm sorry. I should've called. Mom and I went to the movies in Mt. Pleasant. It was late when we got out, and I decided to spend the night at her house. Didn't check my messages until this morning. I almost drove off the road when I heard it was Angela's mom that got shot. They said she's in fair condition and should be okay. I can't believe it. Have you talked to Angela?"

"Not yet. Called her and Zach last night, but neither answered. They were both at the church cleaning up the mess from the other night when it got shot up. Zach finally called me back this morning and told me Angela's mom was taken to MUSC. They spent the night at the hospital."

"This is so bad," Amy said. "Do you think there's anything we can do to help?"

"Not much we can do, at least until we know more."

"Okay," Nick said. "There's supposed to be a news conference at 10:00 a.m. this morning. Hopefully, we'll get more then."

"All right," Amy said. "I've got to get back to work. What time will you get home tonight?"

"Not sure. Zach's been handling the TSA dogs. He told me he won't be in until later, so I'll need to cover for him today. I'll call you this afternoon, but let's plan on hooking up tonight. Hopefully, we'll know more by then."

Nick gave Amy a quick kiss and left The Cup.

~~~

Allen was up early that morning and in his office by 7:30 a.m. He called Heather Wilson. Allen had dated Heather when he was in Washington. She worked on one of the FBI's Evidence Response Teams. There was a lot of fieldwork involved with her job, so she was gone most of the time. They agreed they couldn't keep their relationship going with Allen in Charleston and her on the road so much. They did, however, remain good friends.

She answered on the second ring: "Special Agent Wilson."

"Heather, it's Allen. How you doing?"
~~~

"Same old, same old," Heather answered. "Seems like I wake up in a different city every day. How's the business going?"

"Busy, but good. Actually, that's one of the reasons I wanted to talk. I wondered if you could chase down something for me."

"You mean you're not calling me for a date," she said with a laugh.

"Not this time, babe." His voice turned serious. "You know about the attacks on the black churches here in Charleston recently."

"Yeah, I've heard. Don't know much though."

"Well," Allen continued, "there was another one last night, and the mother of a good friend of mine was shot. They say she's going to pull through. I'm looking into it and just need somewhere to start."

Heather was quiet for a while before answering. "I don't know, Allen. You know how the Agency feels about sharing intel."

"I know, but this thing hit close to home."

"All right," Heather said. "Tell me what you need, but I'm not making any promises."

"I understand. I'm just looking for the name of who heads up a white nationalist group called the Confederate White Knights."

"I'll see what I can get," Heather said. "I've got one person I feel safe asking. But if I strike out with her, that's it."

"Fair enough. Tell your friend I'll give her anything I come up with. Heather, I owe you one. Thanks again."

Allen hung up just as Sarah walked into his office. "So, who's the lucky lady?" she said with a smile.

"That was Heather Wilson, and no we're not getting back together. She's going to see what the Agency has on the church shooting."

"God, I'm just sick about that."

"I know," Allen said, "but at least Zach's with Angela and her mom."

Sarah slid a manila envelope across the desk. "Here's your cybersecurity proposal for South State Bank. Take a look at it when you get a chance and let me know if you've got any changes."

"Thanks, I'll do it now."

Sarah left his office, and Allen began reviewing the proposal. About forty-five minutes later, Heather called back. "Heather, that was quick. Any luck?"

"A little," she answered. "My friend's part of a joint task force investigating domestic terrorism. She concentrates on hate groups. I asked her about the White Knights, and she told me they have individual chapters active in several southern states. All their names are variations of the White Knights of the KKK. The Confederate White Knights is the South Carolina faction, and it's centered in Columbia. She said they've had a recent change in leadership, and the new guy's name is Mason Ivy. They don't know much about him yet. That's all she was willing to tell me, and she wants her name kept out of it. I know it's not much, but I hope it helps."

"Thanks Heather," Allen said. "That'll get me started, and tell your friend I really appreciate it."

All Allen needed was a name, and Heather had just given him one—Mason Ivy. Even an amateur can use search engines like Pipl to dig up personal information Google misses or avail themselves of sites like the "WayBack Machine," which can dredge up deleted websites. Allen was far from an amateur and had been treating the "deep web" like his private pond for years. Everything's out there on the web. You just need to know how to find it, and few hackers were better equipped to do that than Allen Miller.

Allen could now begin to develop a profile of Mason Ivy and his affiliation with the Confederate White Knights. He spent the balance of the morning doing just that. After a quick lunch, he put in a call to Nick out at the Academy.

"Hey, Allen."

"Nick. You hear anything from Zach?"

"Yeah, he called this morning. Angela's mom's in a private room. Zach's going to come out here for a few hours this afternoon before going back to be with Angela. I guess the whole thing could have been worse. The doctors said the bullets didn't hit any vital organs, so she should be okay."

"That's great news."

"Sure is. Did you have any luck with your friend in Washington?"

"Sort of," Allen said. "I'm gathering information on that White Knights group. I also got the name of the guy who heads it up. Let's play 'you show me yours, and I'll show you mine.'"

Nick laughed. "Fair enough. Don't have much but did get some stuff from Steve. There are a couple bars in Summerville and Goose Creek that cater to the white nationalist crowd. The cops are keeping an eye on them. Parrot's the name of the bar in Summerville, and the one in Goose Creek is called the Iron Horse. I figure Josh and I'll spook around both places to see if we can learn anything. We owe it to Angela and Zach. Plus, I'm not sure how much more I'm going to get out of Steve. The muckety-mucks downtown are still pissed about what I did out at Westcott."

"You sure you want to stick your nose in that beehive? I know you two can take care of yourselves, but I'd be careful crawling under the blanket with that racist crew. Those people are dangerous."

"Definitely, but so are we," Nick said. "What else you got?"

"Like I said, I'm still working on it, but Mason Ivy is the guy who heads up the Confederate White Knights. He lives in Orangeburg and is a long-haul trucker. Owns his own rig. About forty-five years old. He founded a white nationalist, Neo-Nazi blog a while back called *The Right Stuff.* His blog hosts a series of podcasts that promote racial purity. They even support ethnic cleansing to make the United States what they call an 'ethnic state.' Crazy stuff. They back the deportation of all non-whites, hate the Jews, and even mock the Holocaust.

I'm surprised the cops or the FBI haven't done anything about these people."

"Yeah, but it's not easy," Nick said. "Remember, it's a free country—freedom of speech, the First Amendment, and all that. They've got to walk a fine line."

"I get all that," Allen replied. "But my line's not that fine when it comes to what I can do on the Internet."

"What do you mean?"

"I'm in the business of protecting people and companies from cyberattacks. And if I'm going to do that effectively, I first have to know how to attack. I don't take it lightly, but if need be, I can be a nasty son of a bitch on the web."

"I don't doubt that," Nick said. "Anyway, if we're going to find out who shot Angela's mom, we need to keep each other posted on what we're doing. Make sense?"

"I agree," Allen quickly answered. "I've got to make a presentation to a bank this afternoon, but let's talk more tonight."

~~~

Zach made it out to the Academy around 1:00 p.m. It was clear he hadn't had much rest, but he insisted on spending the rest of the afternoon working his dogs. Nick and Josh were in the office taking a break when Zach showed up.

"Jesus," Nick said, "we can't believe what happened. How's Angela and her mom?"

"Better," Zach said.
~~~

Nick waited for something else. When it was clear it wasn't coming, he asked, "What do the doctors say about Mrs. Martin?"

"She's gonna be in the hospital for a while. They say she'll be okay, but it'll take some time."

"How's Angela?" Josh asked.

"She'll be okay. Back home now. We'll go back to the hospital tonight."

Nick tried one more question. "Zach, I know it must have been crazy when the church got hit. Did you happen to see anything that would help figure out who did this?"

"Only saw this red Chevy Silverado. Think that was the one with the guns." This was as much as Zach had said since he started working at the Academy.

"Did you see how many people were in the car? Anything else?" Nick asked.

Zach's expression darkened, and his jaw tightened. He slowly stood, and for the first time, Nick saw a side of Zach Brown he'd never seen but always assumed was lurking within him. Zach stared down at Nick and said, "No. I'll take care of this myself." Then he walked out of the office and headed to the kennels.

"Nick, do me a favor," Josh said after Zach was gone. "Remind me never to piss that man off."

Nick smiled. "Just glad he's on our side." His mood turned serious when he said, "I'm afraid Zach's hell-bent on chasing down this thing on his own. And I wouldn't be surprised if he doesn't round up some of his buddies to help. I've seen a few of his black friends, and I wouldn't want to mess with any of them."

"You got that right. So, tell me what you have on these church attacks."

Nick explained what he'd learned from Steve Williams about the Confederate White Knights and the two bars where the members supposedly frequented. "I hate to think what Zach and his friends might do if he finds out about these bars."

"What can we do to help?" Josh asked.

"Well, I say we check out these bars and see what we can find out. If we can get some good intel, we can give it to the department, and hopefully they'll move on it before Zach take things into his own hands."

"Sounds interesting," Josh said with a smile. "Been a while since I've been honky-tonkin'."

CHAPTER ELEVEN

CARLO HAD JUST returned to his room after getting a bite to eat at a Thai place a few blocks from the hotel. He was in the bathroom washing his hands when he caught a glimpse of his reflection in the mirror. Dark shadows encircled his eyes. He saw the world-weary, weatherworn face of an old man staring back at him. The creases and folds marked the roadmap of his life, battered by the years and wrinkled almost beyond recognition. Jaded eyes that had seen too much of the wrong side of the world. He looked away, trying to remember the face of his youth—a face that was clear and strong and had not yet been damaged by the faces of the men he'd murdered. Life is clear in the rearview mirror.

Needing some fresh air, Carlo left his hotel room and found a bench beyond the parking lot under the thick arms of an oak. The evening air had cooled, and the sky turned an ashen gray. Carlo sat, pulled out a cigarette, and lit it with his sterling silver Zippo—the same lighter Vincent Gigante had given him the night he became a made man.

His mind drifted back to a time when working for the mob felt right, when anything but that life seemed absurd. He used to pity those poor souls who woke every morning only to toil at some menial, insignificant job. How many were really happy? How many spent their few hours of freedom each night trying to escape their desperate existence dreaming of the life he lived?

It seemed people have always held a fascination with the gritty, mysterious, and dangerous life of gangsters. Admiration? Perhaps. But probably more about living vicariously, experiencing a lifestyle that rejects the normal, everyday monotony.

That was decades ago, before he came to understand the harsh reality of the life he'd chosen. But he often wondered whether he'd really been the one to choose that life—or had life done the choosing for him.

He was a killer, an assassin, a giver of death. He'd done his job without emotion. His hand had never trembled. He'd never faltered or collapsed under pressure. Yet for all the confidence he had, he now accepted the fact that he could no longer turn his back on the mortality or morality of his life. He could no longer hide from the faces of the men whose lives he'd ended. They echoed through his mind. For the last several years, he'd often wondered what life might be like if he could simply walk away from the mob. But that road had been abandoned the night he took the "oath of Omerta" as the Virgin Mary turned to ashes in his hands. Carlo Tucci was not a naïve man. He knew that the only way out of his own life was probably through his own death at the hand of another—a death most likely by bullet, garrote, or knife.

Carlo felt his life had its own agenda. He was in "no-man's-land"—caught between his past and what the future may hold. He knew there would always be someone waiting in the wings to make a name for himself. Ambition churned strong among crime families.

A few drops of rain began to fall, and the temperature felt noticeably cooler. He stood, dropped the butt of his cigarette on the ground, and snuffed it out.

It'd been a while since his last confession. Carlo crossed himself and decided that it was time for another visit. But that visit would have to wait until he took care of the task at hand.

Back in his room, Carlo watched the fading sunlight stream through the motel window, carving out shadows and sending slivers of light across the walls. Like he did most every night away from home, he texted Sofia. He watched the words "Hi Papa" appear on his phone.

CHAPTER TWELVE

THE BALANCE OF the week passed quickly. Nick and Josh put in extra hours covering for Zach, who spent his mornings with Angela at the hospital. It was Friday afternoon, and Zach had just left the Academy to pick up Angela at the hospital. Nick and Josh were relaxing in the office watching a CNN commentator report on the latest developments in the war in Afghanistan. Josh shook his head. "That fucking thing's never gonna end."

The comment surprised Nick. Josh rarely used foul language and shied away from any conversation about Afghanistan or Iraq. "I had my share of close calls when I was on the force, but nothing like you guys experienced over there. And you had three tours, right?" Nick said.

"*We* had three tours," Josh said, emphasizing the word *we*. "Rocky was with me on every mission. Hell, you know what that dog meant to me. You had Max."

"I know," Nick acknowledged.

A slight smiled appeared on Josh's face. "I remember it was only five weeks into our training, and I knew we had something special." He chuckled. "Shit, we slept together, even showered together. When I ran on the treadmill, Rocky was on the one right next to me running along."

Josh paused at that point. He slowly lifted up the front of his gray Army T-shirt. "The week before our first deployment, I got this." He pointed to the tattoo of a paw print on the right side of his chest. "Hell of a dog."

"I know," Nick said. "Felt like I lost a piece of me when I lost Max."

Josh raised his head, a somber and faraway look on his face. Nick understood Josh was back in Afghanistan with Rocky.

"We were leading our platoon clearing some no-name village with maybe fifteen houses and a mosque when we began taking fire. The Taliban knew how important our sniffers were, and they were prime targets for those bastards. As soon as we were attacked, the first thing that went through my mind was, *Shit. My dog's gonna get shot.* It was a perfect ambush. Bullets coming from in front and from the right. We were pinned down. There was a shallow trench on the side of the road. I grabbed Rocky and rolled over into it, covering him with my body. They tell you in training that it's much better for a dog rather than a U.S. soldier to step on a bomb. The truth is just about every Army dog handler I've known would rather take the hit themselves. The few times we safeguard our dogs are slim compared to what they do for us every time we go outside the wire.

"Honestly, our main job was just to keep them from giving us too much of themselves. It was so damn hot over there, especially for a black lab like Rocky, and I'd have to give him IVs of saline solution to keep him hydrated. He just wouldn't quit working.

"I lost him to a roadside IED in Kandahar. It tore my heart out. The blast busted me up pretty good, but my nerves were already shot. Losing Rocky put me over the edge. I guess I had PTSD before, but I never really noticed 'til I lost Rocky. I started having nightmares when I was recovering in the hospital. I never had those before. He just made everything better for me—that's the best way I can describe it."

Josh's story about Rocky and the war threw Nick back to the night he lost Max, but he said nothing. He knew it was good for Josh to open up.

"I never minded combat. And there was a lot to mind. When you're young you think you can live forever. You think you're invincible. Some guys would puke before going out on patrol. I never did. All that changed after I lost Rocky. After I recovered from my injuries, the Army made me take a medical disability discharge. I wasn't the only soldier to lose their dog, and I'm not talking about just on the battlefield.

The Army contracted with this company called K2 Solutions out of North Carolina. They'd take the dogs when their handler's deployment was up. God, I'll never forget it. Those K2 guys would be waiting on the tarmac when the C-17 landed. Handlers only had a few minutes to say their goodbyes before their dogs were put in a truck and taken away. Didn't make any difference how tough you were—there wasn't a dry eye in the group once that truck drove off.

"Every handler knows these dogs are not just 'equipment,' like the Army calls them. They're battle-scarred veterans who have saved more lives than anyone could imagine. There was a law called the Robby Law passed back in 2000 that was supposed to give handlers the right to apply to adopt their dogs. Problem was this K2 Solutions company would have adoption events where they'd dump the dogs to civilians who had no idea what they were getting. Apparently, K2 was also covertly training and selling dogs for combat and counterterrorism. It was suspected that some of the dogs they sold were ex-military. These poor handlers were given the runaround when they tried to apply to adopt their dogs. They'd been given little to no information and at times were deliberately misdirected. Finding military dogs shouldn't be that hard. Hell, they've all got microchips, and explosion detection sniffers have serial numbers tattooed on their ears.

"That K2 company would have these adoption events. Christ, Nick, these dogs had just come back from war, and many of them had PTSD as well. They were unstable. The people who wanted to adopt the dogs thought it would be cool to own a 'war dog'—a real status symbol. These people were never vetted, never asked what they planned to do with the dogs or if they were capable of dealing with a dog with war wounds. They weren't even asked whether they had small children. Half of these dogs were put on human Prozac or Xanax. And more than I care to think about had to be put down.

"I served with a guy in Afghanistan named Rick Drass. He told me he spent over a year trying to find his dog, Boots. The Army told him to contact K2, and K2 told him he'd have to deal with the Army. He tried everything. Filled out all the forms he got from the Army and K-2. All he got was the runaround. Eventually, he used social media and was tipped off by an ex-K-2 employee that Boots had been adopted by a family in Bethel, North Carolina. Rick tracked them down only to find out the family couldn't handle Boots. They told him 'the dog' freaked out whenever he heard a loud noise. He'd start 'shaking like a leaf' and hide under the closest table. They told Rick that after a week, they'd returned the dog to K-2. When Rick contacted K-2, they told him they had no record of the dog. Sadly, Rick's story isn't unusual.

"The Army supposedly had an investigation about what K-2 was doing, but nothing ever happened. I still feel for all those brothers and sisters who lost their best friend."

Nick put his hand on Josh's shoulder and said, "I know what you're saying. Dogs give us much more than we could ever give them. I'll tell you one thing though. I know Rocky would be proud of how you got your life back together and what you're doing here at the Academy."

Josh smiled. "Maybe so. But I wish to hell he was here with me. No matter how bad things got, he was always there. Seemed like he was saying 'Thank you for being you.' You don't get that too often from people."

Nick patted Josh on the shoulder again and stood up. "I hear you. Listen, do you mind closing up tonight? I've got to pick up Amy. We're driving up to see my dad at the farm this weekend."

"You go ahead," Josh said. "Give your dad my best and have a good time."

CHAPTER THIRTEEN

NICK AND AMY hit some late evening traffic getting out of Charleston but made good time up I-26 and I-77 to Killian. Robert and his Lab, Milo, were all smiles when Nick and Amy pulled into the farm at about 8:30 p.m.

The house was a small white two-story three-bedroom—the kind you often find on farms all across the country. It was showing its age, but it had been well maintained over the years. There was a good-sized barn about 150 feet to the right of the house, its foundation of thick, heavy stone supporting un-painted gray wood walls from countless years of weathering. A puff of the sweet, musty odor of last summer's hay blended with the sharp smell of old metal and machinery. Rays of late evening sunlight filtered through the rafters and played across the old oak beams. Nick drank in the familiar sights and smells of his youth—it was good to be home again.

He was retrieving their bags from the truck when Robert made a beeline to Amy and gave her a big hug.

"Hey, Dad," yelled Nick, "I'm getting jealous!"

"You should!" Robert replied, his arm still around Amy. "It's great to see both of you! Come on in and get settled."

Nick carried the bags upstairs to his old bedroom and then joined Amy and his dad in the kitchen. Robert had just poured Amy a glass of wine and said, "Son, grab yourself something to drink. I've got a fire going out in the pit."

Years ago, Nick and his dad had built a good-sized, raised stone fire pit on the patio behind the farmhouse overlooking the seemingly endless rows of peach trees. And it was nights like this that made the work worth it. The evening was brisk and clear. The night sky was ablaze with stars, the Milky Way putting on a show as it arced across the heavens.

Nick got himself a Coke and made his way to the patio. Robert and Amy were already seated next to the fire pit, with Milo curled up comfortably between them.

"So, how's your world, Dad?"

"Things are good, Son. Pretty much caught up with everything after the harvest."

"How was it this year?" Nick asked.

"Very good. Had the Garcia and Lopez families here again. That's the eighth straight year they've helped bring it in. Good people."

"Yeah, I remember them the year I was back here. They sure were good workers. I worry about them with all the anti-immigration talk going around nowadays."

Robert shook his head. "I'm not sure what I'd do without them. The suits in Washington don't appreciate how important these people are to American farmers. Anyway, enough of that. How's the Academy doing?"

"Busy, busy, busy, but we're keeping up. I think I told you we'll be getting another order for more TSA dogs," Nick said.

"How's that new fellow working out? What's his name again?"

Nick smiled and answered, "Zach. He's great!"

Amy laughed and added, "Yeah, Zach and our friend, Angela, are an item. You should see them together. He's huge and she's so tiny."

Robert chuckled and turned to Nick. "Well, make sure you give my best to Josh, Sally, and Isaiah. You're lucky to have people like that working for you. And how's that computer guy coming along? You told me he got busted up pretty bad."

"Allen's just about recovered from what happened to him out at that warehouse in North Charleston," Nick said.

Robert shook his head. "I still can't get over what y'all went through. I thought those days were over when you left the force. Enough of that. I can't tell you how nice it is to see both of you. Have you two got anything special planned while you're up here?"

"Just relaxing," Nick said. "Thinking of showing Amy where I went to high school. Maybe drive into Columbia, so she can see the USC campus."

"That'll be fun," Amy said, "but remember, we want to spend time with your dad."

"That's sweet, Amy," Robert said. He smiled at Nick and continued, "Thought you two might like to join us for dinner tomorrow night."

Nick sat up straight. "Wait a minute. Did you just say 'us'? Who's 'us'?"

A sly smile spread across Robert's face. "You remember Tim Ryan?"

"Sure," Nick said. "We played basketball together in high school."

"Well," Robert said, "Tim's dad, Samuel, passed a few years ago. Tim's mom, Elenore, and I go to the same church. We've been sort of seeing each other lately."

Nick couldn't control himself. "Dad! You're dating!"

Robert laughed. "Well, Son, I suppose you could say that. Elenore's a fine woman, and I've still got a few good years left in me." Robert glanced up toward the night sky and smiled. "And I'm sure your mother would approve."

Amy was up and gave Robert a hug. "I think that's so cool. I can't wait to meet her!"

Nick was still shaking his head. "I never thought I'd be going on a double date with my dad!"

The three of them spent another hour or so talking on the patio. Finally, Nick checked his watch and told his dad he was bushed.

"You go ahead, kids," Robert said. "Milo and I are gonna sit for a while longer. I'll see you in the morning."

Nick and Amy gave Robert a hug and headed upstairs for the night. Once upstairs, Nick said, "Amy, go ahead and use the bathroom. I'm gonna run back downstairs and get a few bottles of water."

Nick was grabbing the waters from the refrigerator when his dad walked into the kitchen. "Hey, Dad, just getting some water. I think it's great you and Mrs. Ryan connected. And I think you're right. Mom would approve."

"Thanks, Son. Elenore and I enjoy each other's company. Can't believe it's been over sixteen years since your mom's been gone." Robert's eyes went to the middle distance and his voice softened. "Still miss the hell out of her."

"Me too, Dad. See you in the morning."

Nick was leaving the kitchen when he stopped and turned back. "Hey Dad."

Robert looked up. "Son?"

"It's great to be home."

Robert smiled. "Great to have you. And you know how I feel about Amy. She sorta reminds me of your mom when we were young."

"I know, Dad. See you in the morning."

When he got back to his room, Amy had her back to him and was checking out the bookcase full of Nick's baseball and basketball trophies.

Nick admired her for a moment before saying, "You have the most beautiful back I've ever seen."

Wearing a pair of silk pajama bottoms and a cut-off University of Charleston T-shirt, she turned around and struck a movie star pose. "How about the rest of me?"

"The rest of you is just fine," Nick said as he took her in his arms and gave her a quick kiss. "I'll get changed and be right back." He went to the bathroom, quickly slipped out of his clothes, and put on a pair of basketball shorts and an old USC T-shirt. He returned to find Amy under the covers. He flicked off the lights and joined her.

"Still feels kind of funny being here in your bed with your dad downstairs," Amy whispered.

Nick chuckled. "You want me to sleep on the floor?"

"Don't you dare." Amy rolled over and gently laid her head on his shoulder. Nick slipped his arm around her, and they both stayed quiet for some time until Amy finally spoke. "Nick, I know we've only been together a few months, and I'd never put any pressure on you. I just never want to go through anything like I went through with Paul again. I know we've both got our own lives, and I'm not asking for any promises. Just wanted you to know how I feel."

"Listen, Amy, I appreciate what you went through. But I'm not Paul. I'm not saying I haven't done selfish things in my life. Hell, I've done my share. I've let down people I love. We've both learned from our mistakes. I'm not sure what's going to happen, but there's one thing I am sure of. There's nobody else I'd rather be with than you. And I hope to hell I don't mess that up."

Amy held Nick tight, her eyes watering with tears. "Thank you, babe. Thank you."

Nick and Amy made love that night. This was different—quieter, softer, more tender—but every bit as satisfying as it ever had been, if not more. They fell asleep in each other's arms and slept soundly until the night bled away and the first muted light of dawn slipped through the bedroom shades. They awoke still in each other's arms, both understanding that their relationship had reach new depths.

~~~

It was almost 9:00 a.m. when they made their way downstairs. Robert was making breakfast. He stood in front of the old kitchen window backlit by the morning sun filtering through floral curtains. Milo was sitting next to him patiently waiting for any morsel that happened to find its way to the floor.

Robert smiled and said, "Good morning, kids. How'd you sleep?"

"Great, Dad. Something smells good."

"Eggs, sausage, and hash browns comin' up," Robert replied.

Amy took a seat at the old chipped Formica table while Nick grabbed two coffee mugs that had probably lived in the house for thirty years. "Dad, why don't you join us today? We'd love to have you with us."

"That's kind of you, but Milo and I've got to finish up the last of the tree pruning. Also need to tinker with the John Deere. You two have fun."

The weather had cooled, a definite whisper of fall in the air. Nick and Amy spent a lazy morning visiting Nick's high school and the University of South Carolina campus. Amy had
~~~

clear images of Nick as a high school kid and then as a college student ready to take on the world. They had a light lunch on campus at the Russel House Student Union before heading back toward the farm. Along the way, Nick pulled into the Mount Pilgrim Church Cemetery and parked his truck. Amy gave him a curious look but said nothing.

Nick killed the engine and said, "Come on." Once out of the truck, Nick took her hand and led her into the cemetery.

Amy slid her arm around Nick's waist and pulled him close. She understood. "How long has she been gone?"

"It'll be seventeen years next June." He put his arm around her. "Thought it was time I introduced her to my girl-friend." They walked for a few more minutes in silence—taking in the serenity of the moment.

"My mom used to take me for walks through this cemetery when I was a kid. At first, I thought it was kind of weird. You know, walking around with all these dead people. But then she explained how it made her appreciate life that much more. We'd look at the gravestones, especially the older ones, and imagine what life had been like for whoever was buried there. Mom said that those cemetery walks helped her appreciate how beautiful and precious life is."

"Your mom must have been an amazing woman."

"She was definitely that." A moment later, he stopped in front of a simple gravestone. "Hey, Mom. I want to introduce you to Amy. She's pretty cool. Amy, say hello to my mom."

"Hello, Mrs. Giordano. It's a pleasure to meet you."

They stood there for a while, arm in arm, saying nothing, just breathing in the moment. Finally, Nick bent down, cleared a few leaves off his mom's gravestone, and whispered, "We're having dinner with Dad tonight. He's doing good, and the farm looks great. We miss you, Mom."

Nick stood, turned to Amy, and said, "Let's head on back to the farm." They walked back to the truck in silence. As they settled back into the cabin, Nick watched Amy as she buckled her seatbelt. Then he leaned over and kissed her on the cheek. "Thank you," he whispered.

Robert had texted, letting Nick know he was at the John Deere dealership picking up parts. Back at the farm and with a little time to kill before Robert returned, Nick told Amy to get Milo from inside the house and headed to the barn. A minute or so later, he pulled out his dad's Polaris Ranger ATV. Seeing the Ranger, Milo began to wag his tail. He took off and jumped into the bed of the ATV.

"Come on, Amy. I'll show you the farm."

She slid in beside Nick, and for the next hour, they surveyed the sixty acres of peach trees, with Nick explaining the finer points of peaches and how they were harvested.

"I had no idea there was so much to know about a peach," Amy said.

"Yeah, it's a pretty neat little fruit," Nick said. "I always get a kick out of the fact that Georgia calls itself the Peach State, because South Carolina produces almost twice as many peaches as Georgia. We're second only to California. Dad grows what's called 'freestone' peaches. The little pit in the peach is called the 'stone.' They're the kind where it's easy to separate the stone from the fruit itself. These are the peaches you see in produce departments and roadside markets. The other kind is called 'clingstone.' They're harder to separate and are mostly sent to processors who make canned or frozen peaches. The peach originally came from China. Spanish missionaries brought them here in the fifteenth century." Nick smiled and said, "In Asia, the peach pit is considered an aphrodisiac!"

Amy laughed. "Now I understand why you're so sexy!"

"Yep, that's my secret. Love them peach pits!"

It was pushing 4:00 p.m. when Nick, Amy, and Milo returned to the farmhouse. Robert had just finished work on the tractor and said, "I hope y'all weren't out there eating all the peaches because we've got a big dinner tonight."

"We saved a little room, Dad."

"Hopefully that room expands a little bit in the next hour or so. We have a 6:00 p.m. reservation at Saluda's in Columbia."

"Good choice, Dad. Pretty fancy place."

"Well, we've got two pretty fancy ladies to entertain tonight."

"You're right about that," Nick said.

The three of them left the farm at 5:15 p.m. sharp in Robert's Dodge Ram, making the ten-minute drive to Elenore's house, a small three-bedroom brick ranch nestled at the end of a cul-de-sac. It was an older home, probably built in the 1960s. A large live oak graced the front lawn.

Robert pulled in the driveway and parked. "Sit tight, kids. I'll be right back." A few seconds after ringing the doorbell, a tall, slender woman appeared wearing a conservative, dark-gray, knee-length dress. Elenore was a beautiful woman. A bright-red scarf accentuated her shoulder-length salt-and-pepper hair. Her cheeks carried a hint of rouge, and she wore a smile that seemed as natural as a summer breeze. She took Robert's arm, and he led her back to the truck. Both Nick and Amy were out of the Dodge and met Elenore at the end of her walkway.

"Well, for heaven's sakes, Nicholas, look at you. All grown up!" She gave Nick a quick hug.

"Great to see you, Mrs. Ryan," Nick said. "This is my friend, Amy Anderson."

Turning toward Amy, she said, "Hello, Amy. Robert told me all about you. And you're just as lovely as he said you were. And it's not Mrs. Ryan tonight—please call me Elenore."

Robert had the passenger side door open for Elenore, and after everyone was back in the truck, he backed out of the driveway and headed to Saluda's in downtown Columbia.

Located in the heart of Five Points, just steps from the University of South Carolina's campus and less than a mile from the state capitol, Saluda's has been one of the premier restaurants in Columbia since its opening in the mid-1990s. The hostess seated the group and passed out menus. After they were settled, their waiter presented the evening specials, and Robert ordered a bottle of Pinot Noir.

Cheeks became rosier and the conversation more relaxed as the wine flowed at Saluda's.

"Robert," Elenore said, "this is so nice of you. And Nick, before I forget, Tim sends his best and would love to get together the next time you're up here."

"Thanks, Elenore," Nick said. "I heard he's doing great at the feed and seed store. Please tell him I'll give him a call next time we're up at the farm."

Elenore took the stage as she and Amy worked their way through exquisite baked salmon and the men savored prime rib. She wanted to hear everything about Nick and Amy and didn't hesitate to pry a little. It was charming the way she did it, though. Her demeanor, as Nick remembered, was as pleasant as could be.

As the post-dinner coffee was being poured, Nick felt his cellphone vibrate. He carefully removed it, keeping it under the table in the hopes that no one would notice. He glanced at the number. It was Allen, and Nick felt a twinge of concern because Allen knew that he and Amy were at his dad's farm for the weekend. He stood and said he was going to use the restroom. Once inside, he called Allen.

"Allen, what's up?"

"I'm sorry to bother you."

"Don't worry about that. What's going on?"

"Well, I got another call from my contact in Washington. Apparently, the agency believes Mason Ivy has ties to a cartel out of Mexico called Beltrán-Leyva."

"Wait a minute. That's the cartel that controlled most of the drugs coming into Charleston back when I was on the force. I'm not sure exactly what happened, but I know they lost control of the city's heroin and crack cocaine trade around the time I was shot."

"My contact thinks the cartel is planning on partnering with Ivy and his White Knights to make a move back into Charleston. Remember, the drug operation built up by DiMarco immediately began unravelling after he was arrested and killed in prison."

Nick thought for a moment. "That makes sense. There's a vacuum, and you know someone's going to jump in and take control. Stanley Scott said the New Jersey syndicate has already sent someone in to reorganize what's left of DiMarco's operation."

"Exactly," Allen said. "He said the guy's name is Petro or Petrelli—something like that. That means the mob's not going to give up what they had without a fight."

"I'll call you tomorrow when we get back to Charleston. I need some time to get my head around all this," Nick said.

"Listen, Nick. I'm sorry I dumped this on you when you're with your dad. I just figured you'd want to know what's happening."

"No problem," Nick said. "We'll talk tomorrow."

Nick hung up and made his way back to the table. About fifteen minutes later, Robert paid the check, and they all left the restaurant. It was a beautiful night and still early, so Elenore suggested they take a leisurely walk through USC's campus before heading back home.

It had been an enjoyable evening, with Elenore insisting they get together again the next time Nick and Amy visited. By the time Robert, Nick, and Amy arrived back at the farm, it was almost 10:00 p.m. Nick and Amy thanked Robert again and told him how much they enjoyed Elenore and how happy they were he was seeing her.

Once upstairs, Amy grabbed Nick's arm. "Okay, so tell me who called you at the restaurant. I saw you checking your phone right before you left the table."

Nick smiled and said, "Can't get anything past you, can I?" The smile disappeared as he continued. "That was Allen. He told me about some trouble that might be on the horizon." Nick explained what Allen had learned about the link between Mason Ivy's White Knights and the Beltrán-Leyva Cartel.

"So, what's all this got to do with us?"

"I don't really know. But it seems like once you get lined up to give testimony in the trial of a mob boss, you get entangled with some pretty unpleasant company. Maybe like the folks behind these awful church attacks."

Amy squeezed his hand. He could see the concern on her face. "Enough of that," Nick said. "Listen, go ahead and get ready for bed. You've got to work tomorrow, so we need to leave first thing in the morning."

It took some time before Nick fell asleep that night. His mind was trying to connect the dots between cartels, white nationalists, church attacks, and the mob. Amy and Nick were up early Sunday morning and on the road back to Charleston by 8:30 a.m. Nick was quiet most of the way, his mind still in detective mode, mulling possible links between these nefarious groups and trying to determine what to do about them. After he dropped Amy off at her apartment, he went to the Academy and was happy to find Josh, who had been working two shepherds and was about to leave when Nick showed up.

"Hey, Nick. How was your trip?"

"Fun. Nice to see my dad. Glad I caught you." He explained what he'd learned about the Beltrán-Leyva Cartel, Mason Ivy, and the Jersey syndicate.

"I figured something was up with that," Josh said, "considering what happened to DiMarco and his people. But something doesn't make sense. If these White Knights and that cartel are aiming to move in on the drug trade, you'd think they'd keep a low profile. Why the activity lately? And then there's the attacks on black churches. You'd think the police would be all over that."

"Right," Nick said. "But the department's stretched pretty thin these days. Plus, you're assuming these racist assholes are the ones behind the attacks."

"But who else would do something like that?"

"Got me," Nick said. "Maybe it was another hate group. But you're right—it doesn't make any sense. Listen, let's plan on hitting those two bars out in Summerville and Goose Creek tomorrow night. Maybe we'll get some answers."

"Works for me," Josh said. "And we better get some answers before Zach takes things into his own hands. Remember the look on his face when he told us about seeing that red Silverado the night of the attack. I get the feeling he's not gonna wait for the cops to do their thing."

"I think you're right about that," Nick said.

"You want me to stick around and help with the dogs?"

"Thanks, Josh, but you go ahead and take off. I'll close up. See you in the morning."

Nick spent the balance of the afternoon working the dogs and left the Academy at 5:00 p.m.

CHAPTER FOURTEEN

NICK PUT IN a call to Lieutenant Williams first thing Monday morning. Steve had already warned him to stay out of police business, so he needed to be careful how he asked for his help on the church attacks. And he was right. Steve was guarded when Nick told him that the Confederate White Knights could possibly be working with the Beltrán-Leyva Cartel.

"Where'd you hear that?"

"Can't go into it now. But trust me, my source is in a position to know what they're talking about. That's all I can say."

"Christ, Nick, I've told you before, you're not a cop anymore. We'll deal with this shit. If I were you, I'd concentrate on your business and leave this thing to us. Remember what happened the last time you and your boys went rogue."

"Listen, Steve, Angela's mom was almost killed in that church attack. Plus, Allen Miller and I are probably going to have to testify in the government's trial against a mob boss. Believe me, none of us want this shit, but our cards are in the game. You know what Allen can do with his computers, and I promise if he comes up with something the department can use, you'll be the first to know."

"Yeah, but the department knows about our relationship. If anything goes south, it'll come back on me."

"I understand," Nick replied, knowing his next question would make or break the entire conversation. "What are the chances I could meet with Ed Merchant? You can tell him I may have something on the church shooting. I'm sure he'd want anything I've got."

Merchant was the captain in charge of the drug task force back in 2010 and had always felt somewhat responsible for Nick getting shot.

Steve thought for a moment before answering. "All right, I'll call Ed and see what he says, but I'm not promising anything."

"Sounds great. Just let me know when and where."

Lieutenant Williams called back twenty minutes later and said that not only was Merchant eager to get together, he was free for lunch that afternoon. It was agreed they'd all meet at the Hominy Grill at noon.

Williams and Merchant were already seated when Nick arrived at the restaurant a few minutes after noon. It'd been some time since Ed Merchant had seen Nick, and he wanted to learn all about the Academy. After about ten minutes of bringing Ed up to date on his business, Nick said, "Ed, thanks again for seeing me. I'm not sure how much Steve's told you, but I've got some questions about what happened after I was shot."

"Yeah, Steve said you've got some information about what's been happening since DiMarco's organization fell apart. I also know you've got questions. I'll answer what I can, but you need to appreciate there's stuff I can't talk about."

Nick nodded. "I understand. You know I was kind of messed up for about a year or so after I got shot. A lot of what went down back then is a blur. I know the Beltrán-Leyva Cartel lost control of the heroin and cocaine trade in Charleston shortly after I got hit, and the Jersey syndicate moved in. How'd that happen?"

Merchant nodded. "Right. Well, we lost Freeman that night and nearly lost you. You know what happens when we lose one of our own. Chief Taylor pulled out all the stops, and we came down hard on the cartel. It took a while, but eventually we broke them. The New Jersey mob saw the opportunity and stepped right in. They already had their foot in the door with their gambling and prostitution operations in Charleston. It was natural for them to want to take over the drug trade."

"That makes sense," Nick said, "and it looks like the drug business is up for grabs again. I know the syndicate wants to hang on to it, but I also know Beltrán-Leyva wants it back. I have reason to believe a white nationalist group called the Confederate White Knights might be mixed up in all this."

Merchant frowned. "And you think you know this because...?"

"I can't go there right now," Nick answered. "But let's just assume I'm right. What do you know about the Beltrán-Leyva Organization?"

Merchant nodded and said, "The Beltrán-Leyva Organization, the BLO, was started by four brothers in the Mexican state of Sinaloa back in 2008. They became the security force for the Sinaloa Cartel run by Joaquín 'El Chapo' Guzmán. Two of the brothers were killed in 2010, and the organization started to fall apart. That's one of the reasons we were able to take down their Charleston connection back in 2010. However, Hector Beltrán, one of the remaining brothers, was able to reorganize what was left of the BLO and reestablish some of its previous U.S. drug distribution channels, especially in our southern states. The new BLO has evolved into one of the most ruthless cartels we've seen. And yes, they have been known to use groups like the Hell's Angels and the Aryan Brotherhood to distribute their drugs."

"So, you think it's possible the White Knights are in bed with the cartel."

"I'm not suggesting anything," Merchant replied. "Just answering your question."

"What's the department doing about it?" Nick persisted.

Merchant didn't like the question. "Look it, Nick, you were a good cop, and I'm sorry as hell for what happened to you—not a day goes by I don't think about it—but don't think for a minute we want you involved. If you've got information that will help us, I'll take it. You *were* a good cop, but you're a civilian now. So, stay out of it. Understand?"

"I understand," Nick quickly answered. "But *you* need to understand that I'll defend myself if anyone comes after me or my friends."

"All right, let's all take a breath," Williams said, seeing the beginnings of a confrontation. "We're all on the same page here."

Nick could see he'd overstepped his bounds with the captain. "I'm sorry, Ed. I understand what you're saying, and I don't intend to do anything to get in the way of what you or your people are doing. It's just that some of my friends and I could be exposed to what's happening. All I'm saying is that if we learn anything that might help you, I'll make sure you get it. At the same time, if you believe any of us might be in danger, I expect you'll let me know. Fair enough?"

"I can live with that," Merchant said. "I just don't want anyone hurt. Okay, let's say you're right in assuming the New Jersey syndicate, the BLO, and your White Knights group are all players in this thing. All three of those groups are dangerous." Ed sat back and took a deep breath. "Nick, believe me, it's good to see you. You were a damn good cop, and I wish you were still on the force. I know what you went through after you got shot, and I appreciate how you worked to get your life back together. You got a nice business going." Ed smiled and continued, "And a little bird told me you've found yourself quite an amazing young lady. You've come a long way. So, don't do anything to mess that up." Merchant extended his hand and Nick took it.

"I appreciate that. I miss all my friends on the force. You tell them that for me, all right?"

"You got it," Merchant said as they all stood to leave.

Nick laughed and said, "Oh, and Ed, tell that little bird of yours it got it right about that young lady!"

CHAPTER FIFTEEN

NICK AND JOSH closed down the Academy a shade after 6:00 p.m. Figuring that he'd be downing his share of beer that night, Josh left his truck at the Academy and rode with Nick. He suggested they get a bite to eat at the Tattooed Moose before heading out to Summerville.

It was a pleasant evening, and after being seated outside, they ordered ham and cheese sandwiches and had their server bring them sweet tea.

"So, Nick, what's the plan tonight?"

"Let's check out Parrot's in Summerville first and then go to the Iron Horse in Goose Creek," Nick answered. "Hopefully, we can get some more information on the White Knights and this new guy, Mason Ivy. It'd be great if we can learn anything about the church attacks, but we need to be smart about how we do that. The more we learn, the better our chances of keeping Zach and his friends out of this."

It was about a thirty-minute drive out to Summerville, and Nick pulled into Parrot's at about 8:00 p.m. His old truck fit in perfectly with the few other run-down vehicles parked in the pothole-filled gravel lot. The bar itself was a simple cinder block building, its interior pretty much what Nick and Josh expected.

As they walked through the front door, they were hit with the stagnant stench of cigarette smoke mixed with stale beer and body odor. Two men sat at the bar, and another two played pool in the rear of the joint. A good-sized guy studied the jukebox; a skeleton of a woman clung like a spider monkey to his fully tattooed arm. The walls were bare with the exception of a few lit beer signs and a large Confederate flag. Josh nudged Nick and whispered, "Looks like the local tattoo shop had a 'buy one, get one free' sale."

Nick smiled. "Yep, not your typical family gathering place." They took seats at the bar, a few stools down from the two men already seated there. The bartender was watching a rerun of *Duck Dynasty* with the volume off. He eventually glanced toward Josh and Nick. Josh nodded at him and flashed a hand signal consisting of the index and middle fingers held out sideways. The bartender nodded and made his way down the bar to where Josh and Nick sat.

"Two beers," Josh said.

"Miller or Bud?"

"King of beers, my friend," Josh answered.

After the bartender had delivered their Budweisers, he hurried over to a man with a mullet tattooed beneath his actual mullet, who seemed to be attempting to climb over the bar to serve himself."

After the bartender left them, Nick asked under his breath, "What was that thing with your hand?"

Josh smiled and whispered, "I did some research yesterday before our little date tonight. Just gave the guy a Klan hand signal."

They were quiet for a while, taking in the bar's atmosphere—or rather lack of it. A few minutes later, Josh waved the bartender back and asked for a double shot of Windsor.

The tender poured Josh his shots and glanced at Nick. "I'm good, thanks," Nick said.

He returned the bottle to its place behind the bar and said, "Six bucks."

Josh removed a ten from his pocket and told the man to keep the change. "Hey, friend, we're new around here and sure as hell would like to support our brothers and sisters. Anyone we can talk to about helpin' out?"

The bartender ignored Josh and started to walk back down the bar when Josh called after him, "Hey man, just tryin' to keep the faith." This not only got the attention of the barkeep but also brought stares from the two fellows sitting at the bar.

The dude at the jukebox punched in some numbers, and Lynyrd Skynyrd's "Sweet Home Alabama" began to play. The guy sitting closest to Josh said something, but Josh couldn't make out what it was over the din of the song. He cupped his left hand over his ear. "Say what?"

"We don't know you, dude."

"Yeah. Just got into town. We were assuming Charleston still had a few true southern sons."

Josh lifted his right hand to his chest and gave the fellow the same Klan sign he'd flashed to the bartender. The guy smiled—his face lean and angular, reminding Josh of a shark with a switchblade. The smile quickly morphed into an ice-cold stare as he extended his middle finger toward Josh and said, "Fuck off, asshole."

Josh simply smiled and mumbled, "Why don't you take a break and go use the restroom."

The guy slid off his barstool, puffed like a peacock, and took a step toward Josh. "What'd you say?"

The man's breath reeked so bad, Josh had to turn away for a second. Then he downed his double shot. "I said you should use the restroom. Just thought you'd like to use it and stop pissing on the floor to mark your territory."

By this time, everyone's attention was on Josh. Nick grabbed his arm. "Josh, just drop it."

The guy's smile returned, like he couldn't have been more pleased with the way things were going. The bar was suddenly quiet, the tension in the room thick as pitch. The air seemed to crackle. No one moved except the bartender, who reached below and removed a sawed-off baseball bat.

"All right, that's enough," he growled, pointing the end of the bat at Josh and Nick. "You two, out now!"

Nick still had ahold of Josh's arm and was pulling him toward the door. Josh cocked his thumb, gave the crowd a finger pistol shot, and said, "Y'all have a nice night now folks." Nobody said goodbye.

They jogged to the Toyota. Nick backed out, spun around, and punched the accelerator, gravel flying until the tires found purchase.

"Well, that was fun," Nick said.

"Bunch of mouth breathers," Josh said. "Let's try the other place."

"All right, but try to be a little more subtle this time. Remember, we've got to blend in if we're gonna learn anything. Jesus, Josh, sometimes I can't figure out whether you flunked out or dropped out of charm school."

"Got ya, boss. I promise I'll be a good old racist crackerjack this time."

The Iron Horse was about a twenty-minute drive back up I-26 East to the Red Barn exit. Unlike Parrot's, the parking lot was paved and half full with trucks, cars, and a handful of Harleys. The few pickup trucks without a shotgun in their gun rack must have been only passing through or a victim of a robbery. The building itself was larger and looked to be in much better shape than Parrot's. A neon sign carried the name of the bar along with the outline of a horse rearing up on its hind legs.

Nick killed the engine and turned to Josh. "All right, you gonna be a good boy now?"

Josh gave Nick a three finger salute and replied, "Scout's honor."

When Josh gave the salute, Nick stared at the back of Josh's right hand. The number 311 was written in black block numbers. "What's that?"

Josh made a fist and held it up. "I told you I did my homework. The number 311 is one of the Klan's code signs. *K* is the eleventh letter of the alphabet. And three times eleven equals KKK. There's your Ku Klux Klan."

"Jesus, Josh, you're really into this thing. All right, let's split up this time. You go on in first, and I'll follow in about five minutes. That way we'll probably have a better chance of learning something."

Josh smiled and said, "I guess I'm gonna be the canary in the coal mine."

The night air was cotton-thick as Josh left the Toyota and made his way to the entrance. While the inside of the Iron Horse was a cut above Parrot's, Josh was hit with the same repugnant smell of cigarette smoke as he walked through the front door. He felt like he'd stuck his head in a chimney. A bouncer, about the size of an industrial refrigerator, stopped him at the door and proceeded to pat him down—checking for weapons.

The interior of the Iron Horse was larger than the previous bar. The crowd was also bigger and more diverse. But the majority still resembled the characters Nick and Josh ran into at Parrot's. Mixed among the tattooed, leather-clad bikers were a few what you might call "normally" dressed guys sitting at the crowded bar. Several neon beer signs and a few Confederate flags hung on the walls.

Josh saw an empty stool next to a guy wearing a white T-shirt and motorcycle jacket with a "White Knights" insignia displayed prominently on its back. He took the seat next to the biker, ordered a Miller and was taking a sip when he felt a hand touch his left shoulder. He turned toward the touch and found a woman's wax-like, pockmarked face. She wore skintight sequined jeans and a sleeveless black T-shirt cut low in the front—leaving little to the imagination. She had the body of a playmate and a face of a pit bull. She smiled at Josh. He returned her smile, more out of curiosity than anything else.

"What's your name?" she said, her words slightly slurred.

"Josh."

"Hi, Josh. I'm Susie. Haven't seen you in here before."

"Yeah. I'm new in town. Just lookin' for some company."

Susie's right hand found its way onto Josh's knee. "You came to the right place, Jeff." She'd already forgotten his name. She leaned into Josh and purred, "You're cute. Buy me a drink, baby."

Josh figured he could pump her for information. He got the bartender's attention, put a ten on the bar, and pointed to the empty glass in front of his new friend. The bartender nodded, made a bourbon and ginger, and collected the money. He rang up the drink and put the change in the tip jar without so much as a glance at Josh.

Susie picked up her drink and downed it. Her hand again found Josh's left knee, but this time it slid up a bit higher. "Thanks, sweetie." She giggled and slid off her barstool. "I gotta pee. Now don't you go anywhere. I'll be right back."

Josh took a long pull on his beer and turned to the biker seated next to him. "Hey, friend. I saw your jacket. Just got into town and lookin' for a group to hang with."

The guy turned toward Josh. The biker glanced at Josh and then noticed the empty barstool next to him. "I see you met Susie. I'd watch yourself with her."

"Why's that?"

"She's a skanky bitch." He gestured to the back of the room. "And she's tight with the guy playing pool back there. Just watch your ass with him."

"Thanks for the heads up." Josh grabbed his beer and walked over to the jukebox. He noticed a flyer pinned to the wall. It promoted keeping Confederate monuments. Its title was:

TAKE MY CONFEDERATE MONUMENT…WE'LL TAKE YOUR MLK ONE!

He noticed that the name CONFEDERATE WHITE KNIGHTS appeared at the bottom of the flyer. He had just started to read it when he looked up and saw Nick being patted down by the bouncer. He gave Nick a subtle wave and joined him at the end of the bar closest to the door.

Josh smiled and said, "Well, your canary's still alive."

Nick returned the smile. "Good. So, did Tweety Bird learn anything?"

Josh got the bartender's attention, pointed to his empty beer bottle, and held up two fingers. He laid the flyer on the bar in front of Nick. "Take a look at this."

The bartender brought their beers. Nick gave him a ten and told him to keep the change. After scanning the flyer, Nick said, "So, we were right. Looks like this place is White Knights territory."

"Right," Josh answered. He gave a quick look down the bar to where he'd been seated. The biker was still nursing his beer. Then he looked to the back of the room and saw "Skanky Susie" watching her boyfriend shoot pool. "Grab your beer and follow me."

Josh led Nick down the bar to the biker. He patted the guy on his back and said, "Hey, friend. I want to thank you again for warning me about that girl. Least I can do is buy you a beer." He ordered the beer and took a seat. "This is my friend Nick. Nick, this is—don't think I got your name."

"Buck."

Nick shook his hand. "Good to meet you, Buck."

Josh held up the flyer and said, "Wondering if there's anyone we could talk to. We want to help out with the cause."

Buck noticed the 311 on Josh's right hand and nodded. Someone had just put Cat Stevens' song "Wild One" on the jukebox. Buck leaned over and said, "You know that Cat Stevens fellow's a towelhead. Can't turn around nowadays without running into a fucking Osama, black, or Jew. And the government's doing nothin'."

"Yeah," Josh said. "Everyone's afraid of the PC Police."

"Got that right," Buck said. "But I'll tell you, Mason Ivy ain't afraid to tell it like it is."

"I'd like to meet that guy!" Josh said. "Thanks again, Buck. You're a good man. Keep the faith, brother!"

Josh and Nick walked over to an empty table close to the exit and sat down. "Jesus, Nick," Josh muttered. "Can you believe that shit? If stupidity was a crime, he'd be in prison for life."

"Yeah, I know. Buck's not the brightest bulb in the lamp store." They were quiet for a time until Nick happened to look toward the pool tables at the back of the room. His eyes fell on a man leaning against the wall watching the game. He nudged Josh and said, "I know that guy by the Budweiser sign."

Josh turned toward the back, and Nick continued. "He was a detective on the drug task force back when I got shot. What the hell is he doing here?" Nick stood and made eye contact with him. The man must have recognized Nick because he made a slight shake of his head—a clear message for Nick to back off.

Josh also saw the signal and asked, "What's up with that?"

"Not sure. His name's Terry Fitzpatrick. I didn't know him that well, but I can't believe he's part of this crowd."

"I don't know," Josh said, "but he obviously wants you to stay away from him. Maybe he's not a cop anymore. Shit, maybe he's undercover. You can always check him out with your friend Lieutenant Williams."

"Right."

Skanky Susie was still back by the pool table and happened to see Josh looking in her direction. She waved and started walking toward him, weaving noticeably. "Hey there, sweetie," she said when she got close. "Where you been." Definitely high on something, she grabbed Josh by the belt and leaned into him. He took a quick step back, causing her to stumble and fall. She hit the side of the table and ended up sprawled on the floor. She managed to sit up and yell, "Why'd ya do that?"

The entire bar was now fixated on Skanky Susie sitting spread-eagle in front of Josh. The place seemed frozen for a few seconds until one of the guys shooting pool shouted, "What the fuck!" He spun the pool cue around, holding it like a club and started toward Josh and Nick. As he got closer, it became apparent just how huge the guy was. Josh reached down to help Susie up, but she slapped his hand away and started crying.

"You pushed me!" she blubbered.

The pool player, obviously Susie's boyfriend, pointed the blunt end of the cue at Josh and shouted, "Out of my way, asshole!" He bent down and pulled Susie to her feet. "What happened, babe?"

Still crying, she pointed at Josh and bellowed, "Shit, Popeye, he pushed me down!"

Popeye stared at Josh, his eyes flashing like roadside flares. Nick stepped in front of Josh and held up his hands. "Hey man, take it easy. He didn't push her. She tripped. Let's be cool with this. No harm, no foul."

Nick felt Josh grab his shoulder, turned him around, and start pulling him away from the giant. A second later, a searing pain radiated from the center of his back—the pool cue snapping in two. The blow knocked him against the wall and sent a

Confederate flag cascading down on his head. Nick let out a groan and managed to pull the flag from over his head in time to see Popeye staggering back, a fountain of blood spewing from his nose.

Josh stood sideways in front of him, legs bent, fists extended. Popeye managed to right himself, his T-shirt now looking like a macabre Jackson Pollock painting. Popeye lunged forward. Josh bent slightly to his left, and in a flash, his right leg was up and snapped forward—making a sickening sound as it connected with Popeye's neck. Popeye stood there for a second or two before grabbing his neck and dropping to the floor like a sack of potatoes.

No one moved in the bar. Josh slowly backed up, his eyes on the crowd. He reached down and pulled Nick to his feet. "All right, everybody. We're done here. Be cool."

The refrigerator was still standing by the door. He started to move toward Josh and Nick but stopped when someone called out, "Hey, Tony. Let it go." The guy Nick had recognized walked forward, stopping in front of the bouncer. He looked at Popeye on the floor and turned to Tony. "Well, don't just stand there. Help him!" He then pointed to Josh and said, "All right, you made your point. Now get the fuck out of here before someone else gets hurt."

Josh and Nick backed toward the door, and as they slipped out, Fitzpatrick yelled after them. "Come back and you're dead, motherfuckers!"

Josh ran to the truck, with Nick limping behind him. Nick had it started and in reverse before he shut the door. Terry

Fitzpatrick and a few of his cohorts were standing outside the bar watching. Nick spun the truck around and floored it, burning rubber as it fishtailed onto Red Barn Road toward I-26.

Fitzpatrick paid no attention to the other guys shouting obscenities. He stared intently at the Toyota as it drove away, a troubled frown creasing his face.

Nick was almost a mile down Red Barn Road before he managed to speak. "Holy shit, Josh! I hope you didn't kill that guy!"

"Don't worry. Just messed him up a little. Are you okay?"

"I'm still breathing, if that's what you mean. My back hurts like hell. Where did you learn that martial arts shit? Christ, you looked like a ninja back there."

Josh smiled to himself and said, "Graduated from the Army Combatives School before I qualified for K-9. Comes in handy every once in a while."

They were both quiet for a few minutes, dealing with the remnants of the adrenaline rush. "That Terry Fitzpatrick saved our asses back there," Nick finally said. "I still got no idea what he was doing there, but he sure seemed like an important guy with that crowd."

"No doubt about it," Josh added. "I can't understand why he let us go. Talk about being outnumbered. And I wouldn't want to go up against that bouncer. That Fitzpatrick guy definitely recognized you from when you were a cop. I can't think of any other reason he'd let us go like that."

"Right," Nick said. "I'll be looking into that."

Not much more was said on the way back to the Academy. It was almost 11:00 p.m. by the time Nick pulled the Toyota into the parking lot. Josh got out, looked back through the passenger window, and said, "Hey, that was fun tonight. We should do that again soon. What'd you say, boss?"

Nick chuckled. "Yeah, well, I think I'll pass on that for a while. Go home and chill, Josh. I need you out here bright and early tomorrow morning."

Josh pulled out of the Academy. Nick followed and, after locking the gate, headed back to his apartment, arriving there a bit after 11:30 p.m. He tossed his keys on the hallway table, went to the kitchen, and opened the freezer. His lower back was killing him, and without a cold compress, he settled for a box of frozen peas.

Still jacked from the evening's excitement, Nick grabbed a small blanket from the sofa, slid open his balcony door, and took a seat outside. He placed the frozen peas against the small of his back—giving him some relief from the pain. He wished he had Amy for comfort instead of peas, but even so, it didn't take long for his body to unwind in the cool but pleasant night air. Wrapped in the blanket, he closed his eyes and slipped into a peaceful sleep, eventually making it to his bed some time during the night.

CHAPTER SIXTEEN

NICK OPENED HIS eyes to the muted grays of morning. He lay quietly for a few moments, his mind revisiting the events of the night before. He had to admit that his sojourn to Parrot's and the Iron Horse hadn't been all that productive. He was left with more questions than answers. Nothing new had been uncovered about the attacks on Union Baptist or a possible connection between the White Knights and the Beltrán-Leyva Cartel. Hell, all he'd really accomplished was messing up his back. He felt like it had been taken apart and put back together, with a few parts missing.

And what was the story with Terry Fitzpatrick? Granted, he didn't know the guy all that well. But seeing him with a room full of racists just didn't feel right. Then he remembered Allen talking about the FBI infiltrating some of these hate groups. Maybe that was it. Maybe Terry was still a cop—just operating undercover. Nick could ask Merchant, but he'd definitely need to be careful how he broached the subject.

It was 7:15 a.m., and he needed to get a move on it. He felt a sharp pain in his back as he rolled out of bed—a "good morning" from Popeye the Pool Guy. A hot shower and ten minutes of stretching helped relieve the stiffness and pain, and by 7:45 a.m., he was dressed and on his way to The Cup.

Amy wasn't working that morning, but Allen and Angela were seated together at a table by the far wall. After picking up his coffee and muffin, he joined them.

"Looks like someone overslept this morning," Angela said mockingly.

"Tough night," Nick said with a hint of a smile.

"Tough night as in what?" Allen asked.

Nick gave them the short version of the overnight events at Parrot's and the Iron Horse. "Jesus, guys, you should have seen Josh. I swear he looked like Jean-Claude Van Damme the way he took apart this big dude at the bar. I think I'll call him Ninja Man from now on."

"Ninja Man aside, sounds like you didn't learn anything we don't already know," Allen said.

"With one exception," Nick said. He then explained how he'd spotted Fitzpatrick at the Iron Horse. "Doesn't make sense he'd be hanging with that crowd. I'll be looking into it, but I could use some help." Nick asked Allen for a pen. Allen snapped open his briefcase, removed one of his Montblanc ballpoint pens, and handed it to Nick. Nick grabbed a napkin and wrote:

Terrance (Terry) Fitzpatrick
...detective...narcotics...vice...2010...age @35.

He slid the note and the pen in front of Allen. "When you get a chance, see what you can find out about this guy."

Allen glanced at the napkin and placed it and his pen in his briefcase. "I'll take a look," Allen replied.

"Thanks," Nick said. "Did you learn anything else about our friends in the White Knights?"

"No, not really. I've got a business to run, but I'll stay on it as much as I can."

"Right," Nick said. He gave Angela a quick hug. "Give my best to your mom. Tell her we're all thinking about her."

~~~

Nick was on his way to the Academy when his cell began serenading him with Joe Cocker's "You Are So Beautiful," the ring he'd programmed for Amy's number.

"Good morning, Amy. You're looking beautiful this morning."

Amy laughed. "You wouldn't say that if you could actually see me. Was up most of the night studying for my Behavior Management final.

"You up for getting together after work?"

"Sure. I'm going back home to crash after the test. You want to meet at AC's?"

"Got a better idea," Nick replied. "How about I make you dinner at my place? I know how busy you've been lately—juggling school and work."

"That's sweet, Nick. I'd like that."
~~~

"Good. I should be back before 6:00. I'll meet you at my place around then. Does that work for you?"

"Yep. You want me to bring anything?"

"Nope, just yourself. See you tonight."

~~~

When Nick rolled into the Academy, Josh, Zach, and Sally were all seated at the kitchen table, each with a cup of coffee.

"Well, look what the cat dragged in," Josh said with a smile. "How you feeling this morning, boss?"

"Like the Tin Man without his oil can. How about you, Ninja Man?"

"Invigorated?"

Sally chuckled. "Josh was just telling us about all the fun you two had at those bars last night."

Nick poured himself a cup of coffee and said, "*Fun*'s probably not the first word that comes to my mind. But I'm still alive, so that's a good thing. Finish your coffee, guys. We've got a full day ahead of us. Josh, go ahead and give Blue some work in the Shack. Zach, take the rest of the morning with Trooper. I gotta make a quick phone call. I'll work with Rusty as soon as I'm done with that."

Once seated at his desk in his office, Nick called Ed Merchant and set up a meeting at Brittlebank Park, which was on Lockwood Boulevard right across the street from the police station. Nick wasn't comfortable discussing Fitzpatrick over the phone. Plus, he realized he'd have a much better chance getting
~~~

Ed's cooperation if they met face to face. Merchant wasn't happy when Nick insisted that he couldn't discuss it over the phone, but he agreed to meet.

It was a busy morning at the Academy. Nick took a break at about 1:00 p.m. and called Allen. "Did you get a chance to check out Terry Fitzpatrick?"

"First," Allen replied, "how sure are you that the guy you saw is Terry Fitzpatrick?"

"Well, he'd definitely changed. He looked like he lost a fair amount of weight, and his hair was much longer. But he was definitely Fitzpatrick. Why?"

"All right," Allen said. "Got several hits on a Terry Fitzpatrick, but none of them matched your description. Your guy doesn't have an online presence at all. Not just social media—I'm talking about he doesn't even exist in South Carolina's Police Officer Retirement System. I searched the deep web and got no relevant hits. No Terrance Fitzpatrick. I don't know what to tell you, Nick. Are you sure the guy you worked with on the force was Fitzpatrick?"

"Yeah, definitely. Fitzpatrick and Giordano are next to each other in the alphabet, so our names would often be close together on personnel lists, e-mails, stuff like that," Nick insisted.

"Look," Allen said, "plenty of sites claim they can delete your online identity. But believe me, it's almost impossible to completely cover your tracks and become invisible on the web. If this guy is your Terry Fitzpatrick, somebody did a hell of a job doing just that. If he is your guy, then I'd say he's got a completely new identity. Terry Fitzpatrick is no longer Terry Fitzpatrick."

Nick thought for a moment. "Well, if he did go deep cover, that's probably exactly what happened."

"Sorry I couldn't be of more help," Allen said.

"No. This actually does help. It confirms that Terry, or whoever he is now, has probably succeeded in infiltrating one of those hate groups. We were about to get our asses kicked big time last night. He told everyone to back off, and they did. If I'm right, I sure don't want to screw up his mission."

"I'm glad that gives you something to go on. Now, can I get back to my own work?"

Nick laughed. "Yep, go make some money!"

~~~

Nick left the Academy and stopped at Harris Teeter. He bought two steaks, some mixed vegetables and a bagged salad for dinner with Amy.

He pulled into Brittlebank Park—a ten-acre park located between Lockwood Boulevard and the banks of the Ashley River. At that time of the afternoon, the park was deserted with the exception of a jogger putting in a few miles on the path that encircled the park. Nick took a seat at one of the picnic tables, giving him a clear view of the police station. It had been a pleasant day, but now it had cooled noticeably and the sky had darkened. Low gravel-gray clouds pushed in from the north carrying the promise of rain. A distant rumble of thunder could
~~~

be heard, and the wind picked up, rustling the tree branches and sending dried leaves scampering across the ground.

A few minutes later, Nick saw Ed Merchant leave the station and cross Lockwood. As he approached Nick, he made no attempt to hide the aggravation plastered on his face. His demeanor was a clear indication that he wasn't happy. He looked very impatient, as if a minute away from his job was a minute wasted.

Nick extended his hand and said, "Thanks for meeting me."

Ed ignored the gesture. "Yeah, I need to get back. So, let's have it. What's so important you couldn't tell me over the phone?"

"Okay, I know you're busy, so here it is. I was at the Iron Horse last night." Nick paused, trying to gauge Merchant's re-action. A slight tilt of the head confirmed that Ed had an idea of what might be coming next. "And now I'm wondering what ever happened to Terry Fitzpatrick." Nick let the comment hang there. Their eyes locked, and neither spoke for several seconds. Nick finally broke the silence, "Ed, talk to me."

Merchant stared hard at Nick, with that dead-eyed cop thing they all work at perfecting. "I told you to stay out of this. You're writing a check your ass can't cash," he said, his voice not much more than a whisper.

Nick pushed it. "How long has he been under?"

"Nick, you need to back off. Leave this alone. Conversation over."

Ed turned to leave when Nick calmly said, "Maybe I should continue this conversation with Terry." The hook was set, and there was no way Merchant was going to shake it loose.

Ed froze. A few tense seconds passed before he said, "Christ, Giordano. You're not a fucking cop anymore. You could mess around and ruin something big here."

Nick nodded. "You know you can trust me, Ed. I just don't want to be caught in the middle of what's coming."

"What do you mean 'caught in the middle'? You're not part of any of this."

"That's where you're wrong. The woman that was shot in the Union Baptist Church shooting was Cornelia Martin. And one of my guys at the Academy is involved with her daughter, Angela. His name is Zach Brown. He's ex-Army and one tough son of a bitch. I got a feeling he and his friends are going to put themselves right in the middle of this if I can't convince him something's being done about the attacks. Plus, Allen Miller and I are due to testify against the Jersey syndicate, so we're involved, too."

Ed was again quiet for a time. He knew he'd have to give Nick something if he was going to limit his involvement. Finally, his voice again reduced to a whisper, he said, "Yes, Fitzpatrick is in deep cover—has been for almost five years. He's our mole in the white supremacy movement in South Carolina. And yes, I'm his handler. If he's compromised, he's a dead man. Now you understand why he's off limits."

"I figured that much. I also get the idea he may be in the middle of any dealings with the Beltrán-Leyva Cartel." Merchant's silence confirmed Nick's supposition. "How close are they to making a move on Charleston's drug business?"

"Close," Ed said. "We're working with the Feds on this one. We've got some eyes inside DiMarco's old crew."

This caught Nick off guard. "Shit, you mean you've got someone inside the Charleston mob?" Again, Ed's silence confirmed it.

"That's all you're going to get. I've told you too much already."

"Don't worry. This stays between the two of us. You have my word."

Ed quickly added, "And that goes for your buddy, Steve Williams. He knows some of this, but not all."

"All right, Ed, just tell me one thing. Was it the White Knights who hit Union Baptist? And if they did, promise me someone will pay."

"We honestly don't know," Ed reluctantly answered. "But if we find out they did, we'll handle it."

"Just let me know, okay?"

Ed shook his head, stood, and said, "That's all you get. We're done here." He turned and headed back to the station without another word.

Nick was amazed Merchant had given him as much as he had. He didn't intend to do anything to compromise his confidence. But now he needed to figure out how all this fit together. The White Knights…the cartel…the mob…the church attacks. He glanced at his watch and saw it was well after 6:00 p.m. He fumbled the cell out of his pocket and called Amy to let her know he'd be late.

A few moments later, he was back at his apartment building, groceries in hand. He met Amy at the front door, gave her a quick kiss, and they rode the elevator up to the sixth floor.

"So, what's on the menu tonight?" Nick set the grocery bag on the kitchen counter and pulled out the ribeye steaks, cooked veggies, and salad. "Perfect," Amy said. "And how about dessert?"

Nick gave her a sly smile. "I'm sure we can work something out."

Amy returned the smile. "Also a perfect choice."

Nick opened a bottle of wine, poured Amy a glass, and grabbed himself a Coke from the fridge. The rain had held off, and they decided to have their drinks out on the balcony. Dark clouds rolling across the sky shouldered out the sun, turning the world a metallic gray. Night fell gently upon the city—the tops of its church spires losing their distinctiveness.

After they finished their drinks, Nick got up and carried their glasses back into the apartment. Amy noticed that he seemed to be limping a bit more than usual. She followed him inside and said, "Nick, what's wrong? Did you hurt yourself?"

"It's nothing, really. Last night Josh and I went out to a bar in Goose Creek. We got into it with a few of the locals, and I took a pool cue to my back." He chuckled. "I sure wish you were with me when I got home, but all I had was a box of frozen peas."

Amy was not amused. "What were you two doing at a bar last night? It's not like you to go drinking like that." Nick explained they were trying to learn more about the church shootings and a racist group called the Confederate White Knights. "God,

Nick, haven't you done enough? Why can't you let the police handle this stuff?"

He told her about Zach's belief that the cops weren't doing enough about the shootings. They were afraid he'd take things into his own hands. "I figured we could get some information about the attacks and pass it on to the police. But the only thing I got was a sore back."

Before Amy could say anything, he pulled a bowl down from the cupboard and asked Amy to make the salad. He quickly changed the subject. "So, how'd you do on your test?"

"Pretty good, I think. I only have two more finals and a paper due. Then I'm done with my classwork. I start student teaching in a few weeks. Can't wait!"

"What about working at The Cup? I imagine you'll be tied up teaching pretty much all week."

"That's for sure. I've already let my boss know I'll only be able to work on the weekends."

"How's the student teaching thing work?"

"I'll kind of ease into it. The first week or so I basically just observe my teacher. Then I'll start with a few lessons before the holiday break. When I get back in January, I basically take over the class for the next eight weeks."

"Sounds exciding."

"It'll be fun, but a lot of work," Amy said. Then she asked Nick how Angela's mom was doing.

"She's actually doing well from what I hear. Zach's staying at Angela's house in North Charleston to help out."

~~~
~~~

The dinner was excellent, and after clearing the plates and straightening up the kitchen, Amy sashayed toward the bedroom, purring, "Dessert is served."

It was almost 10:00 p.m. when Amy told Nick she'd love to spend the night but better get on home. "I've got to get up early to work on my paper and study for another final."

"Looks like I don't get seconds on dessert," Nick said with a smile.

Amy gave him a peck on the cheek. "You already had a heaping helping."

Nick watched her get dressed and then slipped on his coat. "Come on, I'll walk you to your car."

Amy had parked her VW in the student parking lot, about a ten-minute walk from Nick's apartment. After a kiss goodnight, he watched her drive away—a hint of her perfume lingering like a whisper of spring flowers.

He smiled and started the short trek back to his place. The streets were pretty much deserted at that time of night, but Nick felt an unease settle over him—a prickling on the back of his neck as if someone were watching him. His antenna resonated with some degree of alarm. Then he heard his name called from the shadows of a darkened alleyway. He turned toward the voice but could only make out the silhouette of a hooded figure. He froze as the figure emerged.

"Nick Giordano," the voice whispered.

The face of Terry Fitzpatrick was illuminated by the soft glow of a streetlamp.

"Jesus, Fitzpatrick," Nick said. "You scared the shit out of me."

"We need to talk," Fitzpatrick quickly responded, his voice sounding nervous.

"All right, let's go back to my place."

"No," Terry said emphatically, moving under the awning of a deserted book shop. He wore a black cap pulled low over his eyes. "We'll talk here. No cameras. The Iron Horse? Did you tell anyone you saw me?"

"Just Merchant."

"Anyone else?"

"No."

"What about the guy you were with?"

"That's Josh Taylor. He works for me. He won't say anything."

"Okay, what did Merchant tell you?"

"He didn't have to tell me much. I figured it out."

Fitzpatrick glanced up and down the sidewalk. "What'd you figure out?"

"Come on, Terry. You're underground. Merchant confirmed it."

Fitzpatrick seemed perturbed. "How much did he tell you?"

"I'm sure not everything. But enough. You've been under since shortly after I got shot by that drug dealer. And it's obvious you have pull with that bar crowd. We'd never have made it out if you hadn't stepped up."

"It sure looked like your buddy could take care of himself," Terry said. "And why were you at the Iron Horse? I'm sure it's not the crowd you normally hang with."

"Well, the mother of a good friend was the one who got shot at Union Baptist. I know that bar caters to white supremacists, so I figured I might get some information. Do you know who was behind the shootings?"

"I don't know. They weren't sanctioned by any group I'm aware of. Could possibly be some outlier. No one really knows."

"Some friends of mine and I were involved in busting up that drug theft ring at Mercy Hospital and DiMarco's syndicate."

"I know all that," Fitzpatrick said before Nick could continue.

Nick moved closer. "If you know that, Terry, then you know it's open season on who's going to take control of the drug trade in Charleston. Merchant let it slip that the Beltrán-Leyva Cartel will definitely make a play for it. And word is they're looking to get in bed with Mason Ivy and the Confederate White Knights. The mob isn't going away without a fight, and I don't want to get caught in the middle when this shit goes down."

"I hear you," Terry said, "but the best thing you can do is stay out of it."

Nick was getting frustrated. "Yeah, everyone's telling me to stay out of it, back off, leave it alone. I don't intend to be collateral damage when the cartel and the mob collide."

Terry seemed to sense Nick wouldn't walk away unless he gave him something. He also knew the more people aware of his cover, the greater the chance it'd be blown. "All right, here's what I'll do. I'll let you know what I find out about those black churches, but you have to promise you'll let Merchant's people deal with it."

"I can live with that," Nick said. "As long as someone gets invoiced for that shit. But how will I know what you come up with?"

Fitzpatrick thought for a moment and then glanced at the storefront they were next to: Quarter Moon Books. "Okay, if I get something, I'll call and say, 'I need a good book to read.' You hear that, you meet me here. Whatever you do, stay away from the Iron Horse."

"That works," Nick said.

"And one more thing. You pissed off a lot of people out at the Iron Horse, especially the guy that nailed you with the pool cue. And he knows who you are and where you live. Someone got your license plate number when you and your buddy were leaving. I think you heard us calling him Popeye that night, but his name is Tom Sullivan. He's a mean son of a bitch, so watch your back."

"I appreciate that, Terry."

"All right. But remember, you don't know me." He stepped into the shadows and disappeared into the night.

CHAPTER SEVENTEEN

CARLO TUCCI WAS seated at the Huddle House finishing his breakfast when one of his burner phones rang. He removed it from his jacket and quietly answered.

"It's time to call animal control," a voice said. Then the line went dead. Carlo put the phone back in his pocket, paid his check, and walked back to his hotel room.

At about 1:00 p.m., he drove down Savannah Highway toward downtown Charleston. As he was crossing the Ashley River Bridge, he lowered the passenger side window and, after a quick check in the rearview mirror, casually pitched the burner through the open window. It made a small splash and quickly disappeared beneath the waters of the Ashley River.

Ten minutes later, Carlo pulled his car into the parking lot adjacent to the South Carolina Aquarium. He spent the rest of the afternoon enjoying the wide variety of exhibits at the aquarium and trying to take his mind off his morning phone call. He left a bit before 5:00 p.m., the height of rush hour, and didn't get back to the Best Western until 6:00 p.m.

The La Fontana Italian Restaurant was only a few blocks from his hotel. After enjoying a meal there, he returned to his room. As he did every evening, he texted his daughter, asking about her day. Carlo knew that despite her handicap, Sofia was perfectly capable of taking care of herself. But he still worried about her whenever he was gone and she was home alone.

Most men preparing for a hit would be too jittery to relax, but Carlo had always been able to compartmentalize. He had no feelings one way or another with his instructions to eliminate Frank Petrelli. However, when his eyes fell on the photos of Nick Giordano and his friends that were pasted to the walls of his room, he felt something different. One way or the other, all of the people he'd dispatched over the years were players in the underworld—his world. They all knew the dangers inherent in living the life they had chosen. But these people, these photos on the wall, were civilians. It was strange. He found himself wondering what they were doing this evening—what they were thinking and feeling. Did they truly understand the world they had been drawn into?

He erased those thoughts from his mind as he opened one of his suitcases, removing a knife, a wire garrote, and a Glock and placing them in a small gym bag. He changed into dark jeans, a black pullover, and a pair of black tennis shoes. Carlo put the gym bag in the trunk of the Taurus and left the hotel parking lot. He left his motel room shortly after 11:00 p.m. and turned onto the highway as the dark clouds gathered in the west.

Twenty-five minutes later, he was on the Isle of Palms Connector, passing over the Intracoastal Waterway onto the barrier island. He turned left onto Palm Boulevard and slowed as he passed the Isle of Palms beach villa where Frank Petrelli was staying.

The villa sat dark atop its base of wooden pilings, which lifted the structure into the air, protecting it from the sea. Built in the 1960s, the villa was one of the few remaining vintage single-story beachfront homes. The majority of the older dwellings had been torn down and replaced with multimillion-dollar houses.

Petrelli's Cadillac was parked under the house, and a late-model Toyota Camry sat directly behind the Caddy. Carlo turned the Taurus around, stopped several houses down from the villa, and killed the engine. It was midnight. The boulevard was deserted, the black silence broken periodically by the distant rumble of thunder. Carlo Tucci sat patiently, a constant eye on the darkened villa as the hours passed. The wind picked up around 1:30 a.m., and a smattering of raindrops began to fall.

Fifteen minutes later, a light appeared. Carlo watched a woman descend the front stairs and walk toward the Camry. The parking lights flashed, and a moment later, the headlights illuminated. She backed out and turned left onto Palm Boulevard, heading back to the Connector and off the island.

Carlo waited another fifteen minutes before slipping on a pair of leather gloves and exiting the Taurus. He opened the trunk, removed a twelve-inch stainless steel Buck Knife from the gym bag, and slid it into his ankle scabbard. He then extracted the wire garrote and his Glock 19, shoving the gun inside his belt at the small of his back.

The rain had intensified as he made his way around the side of the villa to a set of wooden stairs leading to a rear deck overlooking the ocean. Once up the stairs and on the deck, he saw Frank Petrelli standing in the kitchen, his back toward him as he filled a glass with vodka.

Carlo tried the deck door and was surprised to find it unlocked. The rain now came down in torrents. Carlo slid open the deck door and stepped inside. Petrelli, hearing the *whoosh* of wind and the hammering of rain on the deck, turned toward the sound. Dressed in only a bathrobe, he staggered backward when he saw the darkened silhouette facing him. His glass shattered on the floor. He managed to right himself and bellowed, "What da fuck!"

Without taking his eyes off Petrelli, Carlo reached behind him and slid the deck door shut.

Frank took a step forward and barked, "Tucci? What da fuck ya doin?" His words were slurred. He was drunk and bewildered. He had that deer-in-the-headlights look as he tried to make sense of what was happening.

Tucci didn't move, drops of rainwater puddling at his feet.

Frank's confusion turned to anger. "Christ, Tucci! You can't just show up in the middle of da night. That shit don't fly with me. Now, get out of here. Ya want to see me, ya call me first."

Carlo calmly walked into the kitchen, picked up the bottle of vodka from the counter, and placed it on the kitchen table. He then grabbed Petrelli by the scruff of his neck, dragged him to the table, and threw him into a chair. He pointed at the bottle. "Drink."

His voice dripping petulance, Frank spat, "I don't want a fucking drink! Ya can't...."

Before he could finish, Carlo slapped him across the face and whispered, "I said, drink."

Frank's shoulders slumped forward. The Weasel had lost his bite. He took a long pull from the bottle and mumbled, "Ya can't do this shit."

"You've become a liability to our friends in New York," Carlo calmly replied. He grabbed the back of Frank's head and slammed it into the table. He moved amazingly quick for a man his size. In a single quicksilver motion, Carlo pulled the garrote from his pocket, looped it over Petrelli's head, and pulled it tight around his neck. Frank tried to grab the wire, but it had already cut deep into his throat. Tucci twisted the handles of the garrote, dragging Petrelli out of the chair and onto the floor. He kicked and twisted violently, but to no avail. After about fifteen seconds, his struggle stopped. His body went limp. Tucci maintained the garrote's pressure for another minute. He then checked for a pulse and found none. The Weasel was dead.

Carlo went to the bathroom and unclipped the shower curtain. He returned to the kitchen, stripped Petrelli, and rolled his naked body onto the curtain. Noticing a small amount of blood on the kitchen table, he cleaned it with paper towels and bleach he found under the sink. However, he knew from experience that it is next to impossible to completely remove all traces of blood.

After making sure that no one was watching, he jogged to his rental car and backed it under the villa next to the Cadillac. Carlo preferred storms when he killed. But when it came time to lug a body to his trunk, he preferred dry conditions. Still, he managed to get Petrelli's down the back stairs and into his trunk. It was approaching 3:00 a.m. by the time Carlo was across the Connector and back on I-526. But instead of returning to his hotel, he headed south on Highway 17 toward the ACE Basin.

An hour later, he pulled to a stop on a small bridge spanning the Combahee River. Swirling beneath the bridge, the dark, muddy water of the Combahee ebbed and flowed with the tides, eventually finding its way to the sea. He removed the body from the trunk and carried it to the bridge abutment. He used his Buck Knife to cut open Petrelli's chest. It would help attract the alligators. Before dumping him in the river, Carlo removed his Glock, placed the barrel in Petrelli's mouth, and pulled the trigger. Should anyone find his body, the mouth shot would be a clear message that Petrelli couldn't keep his mouth shut when it came to the family business.

Carlo Tucci pulled into the Best Western parking lot as morning leaked its gray light spawning a new day. Using the second burner phone, he dialed the New York number. It was answered. "The animal has been removed," Carlo said. Then he

hung up and went to bed, sleeping soundly well into the afternoon.

CHAPTER EIGHTEEN

NICK WAS BACK in his apartment late Friday afternoon and looking forward to an evening with Amy. Charleston was not only known for its rich history but also recognized as one of the country's premier centers for fine art. They'd planned on attending the much-anticipated Art Walk in downtown's French Quarter. Several times a year, more than forty galleries open their doors for an evening of fine art, food, and wine.

After spending an hour visiting several galleries, they headed to Queen Street and Nick's favorite gallery: the nationally known Robert Lange Studios. Nick and Amy were wandering through the gallery, enjoying the paintings, when Nick heard a voice from behind. "Hey mister, keep your hands off the merchandise."

Nick quickly turned around, his frown replaced by a wide grin when he saw the smiling face of Allen Miller. He laughed and said, "Allen. You had me for a minute there."

Allen was with his assistant, Sarah, and her husband, Dave. Allen shook Nick's hand and gave Amy a hug. "You guys remember Sarah and Dave."

"Absolutely," Nick said. "Nice to see you folks again."

Allen was beaming, the wine clearly doing a little something for his spirits. "Nick, I didn't know you were into the art scene."

"Hey, I appreciate fine art when I see it," Nick said. "Just can't afford to buy any. What are you three up to tonight?"

Sarah gently patted Allen on his back and said, "We're helping Allen pick out a painting for the office."

The group spent the next twenty minutes debating which painting would work best for Allen, and they finally, unanimously, decided on a smaller piece by well-known surrealist Nathan Durfee. Amy rolled her eyes after seeing the $4,000 price tag.

They were leaving the gallery when Allen turned to Nick and Amy. "I've got a table reserved at High Cotton. Why don't you two join us?"

"Sounds great," replied Nick. "You sure you've got room?"

"We'll make room," Allen said, and they made the short walk up East Bay to the restaurant. The food was superb, as was the company, and Allen insisted on paying the bill.

"This was fun. I got an idea. Sarah, Dave, and I are going to Boone Hall Plantation next Saturday. It's the annual Civil War reenactment. Why don't you two join us?"

Nick looked at Amy. "What'd you think?"

"Cool," Amy replied. "I've lived here my whole life and never seen one."

"Looks like we're in!" Nick said.

The dinner ended with a toast wishing Amy good luck on her upcoming student teaching. Not a word was spoken the entire evening about church shootings, drug cartels, hate groups, or the mob. After saying their goodbyes and thanking Allen for his hospitality, Nick and Amy headed back to his place.

Nick was about to unlock his apartment when he noticed the door was slightly ajar. He reached behind, holding Amy back. "Stay here," he whispered. Then he quietly eased the door open enough to reach through. His hand found the wall switch and flipped on the light. The place had been trashed—tables and chairs overturned, cushions ripped apart, pictures torn from the walls. The refrigerator and cabinet doors were wide open. Food, broken plates, and shards of glass covered the kitchen floor.

He moved through the living room toward the bedroom. Eying a steak knife on the kitchen floor, he picked it up. The bedroom door was open. He crouched low and eased in, knife gripped firmly in his right hand. After confirming that no one was there, he turned on the light and surveyed the damage— mattress flipped, dresser drawers opened, clothes strewn throughout the room. Then his eyes fell on the empty shoebox and heavy silicon cloth on the floor next to the closet. His Glock 21 was gone.

He checked his bathroom. It was also trashed, the mirror a spider web of lines. When he walked back through the living room, he found Amy was standing in the doorway, her hand covering her mouth. "Oh God, Nick. What happened?"

He glanced at the disaster surrounding him. "Pretty obvious, isn't it? My place got tossed. And whoever did this took my gun."

"This is awful. Is there anything you can do?"

"Not much I can do. I'll call the police. Detectives will show up with a crime scene team. They'll check for fingerprints and other evidence. You can bet they'll find nothing, write it up, and file it away."

"It's like they just came here to destroy everything. Who would do that?"

"I don't know. I've managed to piss off a lot of people lately. I need to call Josh and let him know what happened. Plus, I bet the Charleston mob and their friends in Jersey aren't very pleased with me. Shit, Allen's right down the hall. I wonder if they hit him, too."

Nick jogged down the hall to Allen's place. It was locked. He pounded on the door, but no one answered. *Must still be with Sarah and Dave*, he thought.

Back at his apartment, Nick pulled out his phone and was about to call 911 when he saw the photo propped on a kitchen chair—Nick in his dress blues beside Max. The glass had been smashed.

"Son of a bitch!"

"What?"

He pointed to the photo and said, "They know I was a cop."

Nick called 911. He was told to stay on the phone until officers arrived, which they did about ten minutes later. He then got ahold of Josh and brought him up to speed on the break in. Allen showed up about an hour later. His condo had not been breached.

It was well after 1:00 a.m. by the time statements were given and the crime team finished its work. Nick and Amy were sitting at the kitchen table. Nick looked at the chaos surrounding him and smiled. "Hey, Amy. How'd you like a roommate until I can get this place fixed up?"

"Of course, you can stay with me."

"Thanks, babe. Give me a minute to pack some clothes, and let's get out of here."

~~~

It was after 9:00 a.m. by the time they were up and having breakfast. Nick told Amy he needed to get out to the Academy to help Josh and Zach.

"I'll let Zach and Sally know what happened last night. You should call Angela, so she knows what's up."

"I'll do that," Amy said. "Plus, I still need to finish up my final paper. It's due Monday. What are you going to do about your place?"

"I'll spend some time on Sunday figuring out what's salvageable. Josh and Zach will give me a hand getting rid of what's been trashed. I'll call Mrs. Smyth. She's the lady I rent the apartment from. Plus, I need to take photos of the damage
~~~

and call my insurance company." Nick sighed. "I better get started on some of this stuff."

Amy leaned over and gave him a soft kiss. She took his hand and led him to the bedroom. "No reason to rush."

Nick smiled. "No reason at all."

CHAPTER NINETEEN

THE WEEKEND PASSED quickly, with Nick busy at the Academy and Amy finishing her paper and preparing for the last of her final exams. Nick was on his way to Johns Island Monday morning when he took a call from Steve Williams.

"Good morning."

"I heard what happened," said Steve.

"Yeah, an interesting weekend to say the least. Did you hear whether the crime scene folks came up with anything yet?"

"Nothing as of this morning, but it's still early. The lab will take another day or so. I know the detectives will want to see your building's security footage. I hear you've been busy making some enemies lately. How about you? Any ideas on who might have done it?"

"I'm thinking either the Confederate White Knights or the mob."

"Makes sense. I heard you and your buddy made quite an impression at that bar in Goose Creek. How many times do I need to tell you to stay the hell out of this? People at the department are not happy. Be smart and lay low for a while."

Nick got to the Academy and found Sally was at her desk. "Good morning, Nick. So sorry about your apartment. Josh called me on Sunday and told me what happened."

"Thanks, Sally. I'll be staying at Amy's until the damage is repaired. What do we have this morning?"

"You got a call from Stanley Scott's office reminding you he's flying in tomorrow morning to prep for your deposition. He'd like to meet you at the Airport Hilton at 10:00 a.m. He'll see Allen at 1:00 p.m."

The balance of the morning was spent with Josh and Zach training the dogs. Nick had just finished a quick lunch and was headed back to the kennels when his cell rang. It was Allen.

"Hey, Nick. I got a call from Stanley Scott's office. I'm planning on being at the Hilton at noon. I thought we could meet for lunch before my one o'clock meeting with him."

"Sounds like a plan. I'm glad you called. I got the name of one of the guys Josh and I ran into the other night at the Iron Horse. Tom Sullivan. Hoping you could check him out for me. There's a chance he's one of the guys who tossed my place Friday night."

"Christ, Nick. How many times have I told you to put a security system on your apartment? Any monkey with a credit card could get into your place."

"I know, I know," Nick said. "I'll take care of it. Now, do you think you could check out Sullivan?"

"You got it. Are you up to anything after work?"

"Not really. I'm staying at Amy's until I can get back into my apartment. Why? What's up?"

"I thought we could get together. We can talk about the deposition stuff, plus I may have something on your Sullivan fellow."

"That'll work. Amy's going to be busy studying for one of her finals. I should probably get out of her hair. What time do you want me to stop by?"

"How about around 6:00 or 6:30?"

"I'll be there. Thanks, Allen."

~~~

Nick made it to Allen's condo around 6:30 p.m.

"Come on in," Allen said. "Want a beer?"

"How about a Coke?"

"Absolutely." Allen got the drinks, and they sat down at the kitchen table. "So, what do you think about the depositions?" Allen asked.

Nick thought for a moment and then said, "I was thinking about that. I imagine they'll be pretty straightforward. I remember when we met Mr. Scott and his assistant last month. They made it pretty clear that what you and Sarah discovered about Mercy and Westcott may not be admissible in court."

"I know," Allen said. "I was thinking the same thing. But we'll just have to wait and see what Rossini's lawyer says on Wednesday. Scott said this Bryson guy is supposed to be pretty sharp. I did some research on him after our meeting. This guy
~~~

is the real deal. Grew up in New York City—rich and powerful parents, summers in the Hamptons, private schools, the whole nine yards. Did his undergraduate at Dartmouth and was first in his class at Harvard Law School. He worked at the U.S. Attorney's Office for about ten years after he graduated and developed quite a reputation prosecuting organized crime. There was even talk he was in line for the assistant U.S. attorney's job in Washington. Then he up and leaves his government job and starts his own law firm. Now he does a complete 180 and starts working for the same type of people he used to prosecute. That's when he hooked up with Rossini."

"Sounds like a heavy hitter," Nick said. "Hey, did you have any luck finding anything on Tom Sullivan?"

A conspiratorial grin spread across Allen's face. "You mean your buddy, Popeye Sullivan?"

Nick chuckled. "He's not my buddy. And how'd you know everyone calls him Popeye?"

"I wish I could say it was my amazing computer skills," Allen said, the smile getting even broader. "Truth is I got lucky. Just looked up his Facebook page. For some reason, he left his timeline setting on public, so anyone can see it. Not smart. Turns out old Popeye Sullivan's quite a colorful dude. Makes no bones about his view of blacks, Jews, and anyone else who's not lily-white. He owns a small moving company in Goose Creek. I got his home address in Summerville and the address of his company."

"Sounds like I could have found this stuff out if I had the time," Nick said. "What else you got?"

Allen reached back, grabbed a sheet of paper from the kitchen counter, and handed it to Nick. "I pulled this photo of Tom Sullivan from his Facebook page. Plus, I wrote the addresses of his house in Summerville and his Goose Creek moving company on the back of it."

"Thanks." Nick studied the addresses on the back of the photo. "At least now we know where he lives. You'd think the cops would be all over this guy, but I'll give them a copy of the photo."

"Good idea. So, once I got some basic information on Sullivan, I decided to take another run at Mason Ivy. I accessed his computer through his *Right Stuff* blog and lifted some of its browser cookies. Like most people, he doesn't bother getting rid of them, which was fortunate for me, because they contain a lot of information. He also hadn't cleared his browser history, so I checked out what sites he's visited and dug into his e-mail, too."

Nick shook his head. "I still can't believe the shit you can do with your computers. What'd you find?"

"A lot," Allen said. "Seems like our friend has been spending a fair amount of time researching Mexican drug cartels and the mafia."

"That's about what we'd expected," Nick said.

"Exactly," Allen said. "So, get this. I'm trolling his e-mails and find out he sometimes uses ProtonMail. That's an encrypted e-mail provider that's almost impossible to crack. There's a good chance that Ivy's using this to communicate with the cartel. And there's been a sharp increase in the number of encrypted e-mails over the past week."

"If the cartel's going to make a move, sounds like it'll happen soon," Nick said. "As a matter of fact, I may be able to get more information on that."

"How?"

Knowing he couldn't talk about his conversations with Merchant or Terry Fitzpatrick, Nick said, "Can't tell you, but I'll let you know what I find out."

~~~

The actual depositions on Wednesday were held at the U. S. Attorney's Office on Meeting Street. Phillip Bryson already had the interrogatories and other information.

Nick's deposition began smoothly, with Bryson spending about a half hour questioning Nick about his education, his career as a police officer, and the Academy. The only contentious moments came when Bryson probed Nick about the night he was shot in North Charleston and the following year, which ended with his resignation from the force.

"I understand you were shot the night of August 12, 2010."

"That's correct," Nick answered.

"And am I correct that you initiated the raid on a suspected drug house on the night in question?"

"Correct," Nick responded.
~~~

"And am I correct that an officer named James Freeman died during your attempt to arrest a Beltrán-Leyva Cartel operative by the name of Mr. Luis Ramirez that night?"

"Yes."

"When you made the decision to proceed with the raid, did you request and wait for backup prior to entering the subject's premises?"

"Yes, I called in a Code 8 requesting cover and backup."

"And that's when Officer Freeman arrived on the scene?"

"That's correct."

"All right. After Officer Freeman arrived, did you call in a Code 966, indicating a drug bust was in progress?"

"Yes, I did."

"And would you say it's standard departmental operating procedure to wait for additional backup prior to initiating raids?"

"Generally, yes. But the primary officer on the scene can make a decision to proceed without additional backup."

"And you made that decision?"

"I did."

"And Officer Freeman was shot and killed after you entered the suspect's house?"

"Yes, he was."

"Let me ask you this, Mr. Giordano: Was it prudent to proceed without additional backup? Did you make the right decision?"

Nick knew this was coming. He let the question hang and then answered, "No. In hindsight, my decision to move forward without the support of additional officers was not a prudent one."

"Are you saying you made a mistake in judgement?"

"Yes, I'm saying I made a mistake."

Phillip Bryson stared at Nick for a moment before continuing. "I also understand your police dog was killed that night. Correct?"

Nick shut his eyes and tried to calm himself. He'd expected to be grilled about Freeman's death but hadn't prepared himself for questions about Max. His answer was not much more than a whisper. "Yes, Max was shot."

"Excuse me," the stenographer said. "Could you please repeat your answer?"

Feeling the pressure, he snapped. "I said my dog, Max, was shot and killed!" Then he took a deep breath to steady himself. "I'm sorry."

The room was quiet. "I realize this may be difficult, Mr. Giordano," Bryson said. "Would you like to take a few minutes?"

Nick sensed a hint of condescension. "No," he answered curtly.

"All right," Bryson said. "Let's continue. I understand you had a somewhat difficult year following the shooting." Nick said nothing. Bryson pushed forward. "Would you say that was true, Mr. Giordano?"

"It was a difficult time, but I dealt with it."

"And in dealing with it, would you say you began to use alcohol to an excess?"

"I'm not going to deny it. I made the mistake of thinking alcohol could help me deal with the aftermath of the shooting. I was wrong, but I worked through it."

"Would you say your drinking affected your ability to carry out your duties as a police officer?"

Nick was growing impatient. "I think I just said that, Mr. Bryson."

"Yes," Bryson quickly responded. "You did say that, didn't you? Would you also say that your drinking was partly responsible for your resignation from the police department?"

"Yes, that was one reason."

Bryson kept the pressure on. "And what were the other reasons, Mr. Giordano?"

"All right, that's enough," Scott objected. "You've established Mr. Giordano had a difficult time after the shooting. So, move on."

Bryson simply smiled. "Fair enough. Let's move on then. Is it true that after you resigned from the police department, you required psychiatric help from a Dr. Judith Bailey?"

Nick again paused before answering, "I would say I was experiencing some level of depression. And yes, Dr. Bailey help me deal with that."

The balance of the deposition dealt with Nick's involvement with Allen and how it pertained to Mercy General Hospital and Westcott Distributing.

Bryson was successful in establishing several facts. First, Nick had made questionable decisions the night of his shooting. Second, he used alcohol to an excess and required psychiatric care. Third, he had no direct contact with Mario Rossini. Finally, he was the first to fire his weapon at the Westcott warehouse, therefore initiating the subsequent use of force by DiMarco and his associates.

~~~

Allen's deposition began much like Nick's. Bryson had a variety of questions concerning Allen's education, his work at US-CERT, and his company, CyberNet Security. He spent a fair amount of time questioning Allen on his computer and technological capabilities, specifically the techniques he used to bypass firewalls in order to access internal operating systems.

But then Bryson got down to business. "Mr. Miller," Bryson began, "tell me how you first became involved with Mercy Hospital." Allen gave a general account of how and when he was contacted by Mr. Jack Rennells, the CEO of Mercy Hospital's parent company, MediGroup. He explained what he was asked to do and how he went about accomplishing it.

"So, let me see if I've got this straight," Bryson said. "You were hired to hack into corporate files owned by Mercy Hospital and its parent company, MediGroup. Correct?"

"Yes," Allen said, "that's one way of putting it."

"And am I correct in assuming your authority to hack these files would be limited to those existing within the company's internal systems?"

"That would be correct."
~~~

"All right. So, you weren't authorized to access employee information that existed outside company files?"

Again, Allen was expecting this. "That would not be part of my mandate."

"I see," said Bryson, emphasizing the fact with his next statement. "So, you're saying you would have no legal right to access an employee's personal files if those files existed outside the company?"

"That is correct."

"Interesting," Bryson said. "Are you familiar with the Computer Fraud and Abuse Act of 1986?"

"Yes."

"Mr. Miller, are you familiar with section 1030 of the federal criminal code, which makes unauthorized access into a protected network or computer a federal crime?"

"Yes."

"Thanks for clarifying. Now, have you ever hacked a Mercy employee's personal computer?"

"Yes."

"Have you ever hacked into the company computers at Westcott Distributing?"

"Yes."

The rest of the deposition covered Allen and Sarah's involvement in uncovering the theft of narcotics from Mercy and its connection to Westcott. Allen's deposition wrapped up around 4:30 p.m.

Stanley Scott had arranged to meet Nick and Allen afterward at the U.S. Attorney's Office to debrief the depositions.

"Gentlemen," Scott began, "I think both of you did a good job. Your answers were succinct and honest."

"Yeah," Nick said, "but Bryson sure hit me hard about how I handled the shooting and the problems I had getting my life back on track."

"I told you that was to be expected," Scott said. "He'll use that to discredit you should you testify during the trial."

"And he sure nailed me on how I got most of my information," Allen added.

"Again," Scott said, "we expected that, too. The more Bryson can discredit Nick and argue that your findings are inadmissible, the greater his chance of winning the case."

"Well," Nick said, "it sure sounds like he did a great job on both counts."

"You may be right," Scott said. "But like I said, both of you did an excellent job and will be effective witnesses if you're required to testify. In any case, the trial is months away—a lot can happen between now and then. My advice would be to get on with your lives and let us worry about what comes next."

Stanley Scott and Ms. White stood and were getting ready to leave when Nick said, "One more thing. When we met last month, you told us we might be in danger based on what we know about DiMarco and the mob. After today, do you think that's still the case?"

"Good question," Scott replied, "What do you think, Jennifer?"

Jennifer White thought for a moment. "Based on today, I'd say both of you have less to worry about. However, I recommend you don't get complacent. Like Stanley said, things can change over the next few months. If I had to guess, I'd say Allen presents more of a risk to Rossini than you, Nick."

Allen laughed, "Well, that's comforting!"

Scott patted him on the back and said, "Don't hesitate to call either of us if you have any questions. But now we need to catch a plane back to New York."

CHAPTER TWENTY

BRYSON'S DRIVER, ISAAC, picked him up on Thursday morning and took the Holland Tunnel out of Manhattan into Jersey City. A short while later, the Cadillac eased to a stop in front of Antonio's.

"Thank you, Isaac," Bryson said. "You can wait here. Shouldn't be too long."

At that hour, the bar was empty with the exception of the bartender and a rather large man seated beside the stairs leading to the second-floor social club. The man was reading a Michael Connelly paperback. Without raising his eyes, he said, "He's expecting you." Bryson nodded and proceeded up the stairs.

Mario Rossini was on the phone when Bryson entered. He saw Phillip and pointed to a chair across from him.

"I understand. I agree it was necessary. I'm going to have to call you back. Bryson's here." He hung up. "So, tell me about Charleston." Bryson reviewed both depositions—highlighting the key points accomplished in each.

"So, do we have a problem or not?" asked Rossini.

"Possibly, but not likely."

"I don't like the word *possibly*. Explain."

"Regarding Mr. Giordano, the dog trainer, I established he had no direct contact with you or any of your people outside Charleston. I doubt Scott will even use him if this gets to trial. Even if he does, I'll have no problem discrediting him on the stand. Allen Miller may be another story."

"How so?"

"The majority of what Miller discovered was done so illegally. No judge will allow any of his testimony concerning Westcott to be admitted."

"The 'majority'? What the hell does that mean?"

"Some of what Mr. Miller uncovered from Mercy General's internal computer files could possibly be admissable. He was given authority to access those files by top management. This, however, would be limited to what he learned about DiMarco's scheme to remove narcotics from the hospital. As I said, nothing regarding Westcott will be admissable."

Rossini frowned and leaned forward. "You used the word *possibly* again, Phillip. 'Possibly' is not acceptable. What else do you have?"

"I'm going to have to go back to Charleston. The Miller and Giordano depositions were set up before I received all the interrogatories I requested. They show that Miller's assistant was much more deeply involved than I first thought."

"What's his name?" asked Rossini.

"It's a she—Sarah Pryor."

At that point, Sal Ruggiero appeared, nodded toward Phillip, and took a seat next to Mario.

"All right, Phillip," Rossini said. "Do whatever you need to do. I don't want any surprises. Understood?"

It was a cue for him to leave. "Yes, sir," Bryson said and then made his way down the stairs.

Sal shut the door and asked, "So, what'd he say?"

Mario brought him up to speed. "Looks like I might still be exposed if this Miller guy and his assistant testify. Who's Tucci dealing with in Charleston?"

"He's pretty much on his own," Ruggiero said. "Petrelli gave him some information on the players down there. Carlo's been in contact with Trantino and Esposito. He knows Trantino's gonna take over running our loan business down there. The Esposito kid's only a cugine, but Trantino likes him and put him in charge of reestablishing our drug connections."

Rossini turned away from Sal as a dark silence engulfed him. After a moment, he got up and walked to the bar, thinking about how best to handle the situation. Even though it was midmorning, he poured himself two fingers of Glenfiddich and returned to the sofa. He never asked Ruggiero if he wanted a drink. "Forget about Petrelli. He's not a factor anymore."

"What'd ya mean?" Sal asked. "I thought you said New York wants Petrelli to run Charleston's money through Florida?"

Mario stared at Sal. "You got a hearing problem, Sal? I said forget about Petrelli. You set up Tucci down there, right?"

"Yeah. I gave him bogus creds—different name, driver's license, credit card. Stuff like that. Why? You want that I should get ahold of him?"

"No," Mario quickly answered. "I'll handle it myself. Now get out of here. I need to think."

Sal Ruggiero was taken aback. It wasn't like Mario to jump all over him. But he figured he best just leave him alone. "All right, all right. I got things to do anyway," Sal said. "Call me when you need me."

Sal was leaving the room when Mario called after him, "And shut the fucking door."

Mario got up and started pacing. He had to weigh the risk of eliminating certain people in Charleston with the chance their testimony could "possibly" implicate him. Bryson had said their testimony would most likely be inadmissable in court. But could he take that chance? He thought of his associates who had been done in after their lawyers used the word *possibly*. A moment later, he went to the wall cabinet and pulled out one of a dozen burners. He dialed the New York number. He would need permission to do what he was about to do.

~~~

It was after 11:00 p.m. Thursday evening. Carlo Tucci was outside his hotel room having a smoke before going to bed. He felt the vibration and removed the remaining burner phone given to him by Liborio Bellomo.

"Yes."
~~~

"Have you identified Allen Miller and his assistant?"

"Yes."

"Burn them both. Make it clean. Do it now." The phone went dead.

Tucci drop the burner, stepped on it, and put the remains in his coat pocket. He would get rid of it later—far from his hotel.

CHAPTER TWENTY-ONE

ANGELA AND ALLEN had already arrived at The Cup Friday morning when NIck showed up. He picked up his muffin and coffee, waved at them, and headed over to their table.

Nick took a seat next to Allen and said, "TGIF, my friends!"

"Well," Allen said, "you're pretty chipper for someone whose apartment just got trashed."

Nick smiled. "Yeah, well, I'm staying at Amy's place, so it can't be all bad."

Angela said, "So, what do you guys have going on this weekend?"

"A group of us are going to the Civil War reenactment out at Boone Hall Plantation on Saturday," Allen said. "I went to one of those when I was a kid. Had a ball. The one this Saturday's a reenactment of the Battle of Secessionville, which took place out on James Island in 1862. The Confederates won that one. The people in these reenacments put on quite a show. Hundreds of people from all over show up to participate. There's muskets, cannons, horses—pretty authentic stuff."

Angela shook her head and said, "Well, a lot of folks 'round here don't seem to mind pretending that the South won a war they lost."

"Why don't you and Zach join us?" Allen said.

"Sounds like fun, but we're taking Mom to church tomorrow. It's her first time back there since she got shot. The congregation is having a special service for her."

"Well, we'll miss you guys," Nick said, "and please give your mom our best. I need to get going. Josh is delivering two of our dogs to Atlanta Tuesday, and I've got to finish the paperwork. Allen, I'll see you later, but let's plan on leaving about 9:30 or so tomorrow morning. Amy and I'll pick you up. Go ahead and arrange a place for us to meet Sarah and Dave. The reenactment starts at 11:00, and you know the place will be packed."

Allen and Angela left The Cup a few minutes later.

~~~

Carlo Tucci remove the earbuds, disconnected his listening device, and sat quietly for the next few minutes considering what he'd just heard. His orders were clear: two people needed to be terminated, and it needed to be done quickly. Carlo was concerned—not so much with the assassinations themselves, but
~~~

rather with the urgency of them. His hits had always been meticulously planned, never rushed. But if they had to be done quickly, at least now he knew his cover and how and when it would go down.

CHAPTER TWENTY-TWO

ALLEN WAS WAITING outside when Nick and Amy arrived at 9:30 a.m. on Saturday. Allen slid into the back seat of the truck. "I told Sarah and Dave we'd meet them at the ticket booth."

It was about a forty-minute drive to Boone Hall, which was located eight miles north of downtown Charleston in Mt. Pleasant. Cars were backed up on Highway 17 leading up to the plantation. As they were waiting in line, Amy mentioned that even though she'd grown up in Mt. Pleasant, she'd never taken a tour of the plantation.

"Well, I did a little research last night," Allen said. "Boone Hall is one of the oldest plantations in the country. It was founded in 1681 when Major John Boone came to Charleston from England. He built the plantation on the banks of Wampacheone Creek so he could barge his cotton crop to Charleston. It covers almost 750 acres. It's famous for its long oak-covered road called the "Avenue of the Oaks" and its ten-thousand-square-foot antebellum mansion. And you've probably seen it in the movies. The miniseries *North and South*, Alex Haley's *Queen* and *The Notebook* were filmed here. So, there's your history lesson for today."

After a twenty-minute wait, Nick finally pulled in and found a parking spot. Amy was amazed at the sheer number of people pouring into the grounds. They made their way to the ticket counter and met up with Sarah and Dave. A ten-minute walk brought them to a huge open area where the majority of the reenactment would take place. Once they found a good spot, Amy laid a blanket down in front of the roped barrier separating the spectators from the participants, and everyone got situated. The actual reenactment would start in about thirty minutes, giving Nick and Dave time to buy drinks and snacks for the group.

"This is great," Sarah said. "I bet there must be a couple thousand people here already."

Three good-sized wheeled cannons were lined up not far from where they were seated. Large groups of musket-carrying Confederate and Union soldiers were beginning to gather. Several were on horseback. Excitement was building.

Shortly after 11:00 a.m., groups of Union and Confederate soldiers approached each other on horseback at the center of the field. After meeting for a few minutes, they broke apart and galloped back to their respective sides. A moment later, a Union soldier set off one of the cannons. Billows of smoke poured from the mouth of the cannon followed by an ear-shattering boom. For the next thirty minutes, both sides exchange cannon fire. Lines of soldiers fired their muskets, reloaded, and fired again. Several soldiers acted as if they'd been shot and fell on the battlefield.

After a half hour of action, the shooting stopped. Several individuals dressed in Civil War garb mingled through the crowd, explaining what had just happened and how the battle would progress. Sarah and Dave wandered off to check out the booths displaying a wide variety of Civil War memorabilia.

They returned, and the group settled in for the next round of action. This time, rows of soldiers assembled in the field, stopping about 150 feet from each other. Men in the front rows were down on one knee, while those in the back rows stood behind them. The end lines of the soldiers were suprisingly close to where Nick and his friends were seated. Then a cannon fired, announcing the next round of the battle.

The crackle of muskets filled the air as the rows of soldiers started firing. The action continued as the soldiers fired and reloaded—many of them grabbing their faces or chests as if shot.

Then another cannon fired to the right of the group. Nick quickly turned his head toward the sound and noticed a large man standing about fifteen yards away. The man wore sunglasses and a black baseball cap. His attention was focused on Nick. A jacket was draped over his left forearm. Nick noticed a black object protruding from under the jacket. At that moment, both lines of soldiers fired, the sound of muskets resounding through the crowd. Nick saw the muzzle flash spit from the end of the man's gun. Without thinking, he dove forward, crashing into Amy and Allen. The man fired two more shots from under his jacket, their sound drowned out by the musket fire.

Amy tumbled to the ground with Allen and Nick sprawled on top of her.

Allen righted himself and muttered, "Jesus, Nick. What the hell?"

Nick jumped to his feet and looked toward the man with the jacket. He was gone. He turned back to see Sarah on her side, holding her right arm. Blood began to ooze from between her fingers, darkening her white blouse. Dave saw the blood and was at her side, trying to comprehend what had just happened.

The musket fire had drowned out the gunshots, and people around Nick were unaware of anything out of the ordinary until a woman pointed at Sarah and shouted, "Oh my God!"

Attention was quickly drawn to Sarah, and panic spread throughout the crowd. A man got the attention of two security personnel, who immediately radioed for help.

Dave was consoling Sarah, telling her that it was going to be okay, although his frightened look didn't match his tone. Nick inspected the wound and realized that the bullet had only grazed her arm right below the shoulder.

"Sarah, stay put," Nick said. "Help will be here soon. You're going to be all right."

"It stings," Sarah said through clinched teeth.

Word spread through the crowd. People were wondering if it had been a reenactment-related incident. Someone yelled, "Jesus, did some idiot actually load live ammunition?"

A few minutes after the shooting, the EMT van that had been parked at the entrance to the event pulled up. It was followed by three policemen. Sarah was helped into the van. Dave jumped in behind her, and the the cops cleared a path through the gathering crowd so the van could take off for MUSC. The balance of the reenactment was suspended for several hours.

More police arrived, and the area around the shooting was cleared. When the police asked what they had witnessed, Allen and Amy were at a loss. But Nick was able to give a general description of the man with the sunglasses and baseball cap and confirm that he was the shooter.

Once the area was cordoned off, Nick, Amy, and Allen provided their formal statements and were allowed to leave for MUSC around 3:00 p.m. They arrived at the hospital and were ushered into the emergency room waiting area, where they found Dave pacing.

"She's doing okay," he said. "Luckily, it was just a flesh wound. There was a lot of blood, but the doctor said her injury is relatively minor."

"Thank God," Allen said. "Sorry we couldn't get here sooner, but the cops had us tied up."

"I understand. Two detective showed up here, and I told them what I saw, which was basically nothing. What happened out there?" Nick gave an abbreviated recap of what he'd seen. "Does anyone know who the guy was?" Dave asked.

"I was the only one that got a look at him. Never seen him before."

At that moment, an interior emergency room door opened, and Sarah appeared with a young doctor. Dave gave her a hug, careful not to bump her arm, which was bandaged and in a sling.

The doctor shook Dave's hand and introduced himself. "Keep her arm immobilized and in the sling for the next few days. The stitches can come out in seven to ten days." The doctor handed Dave a sheet of paper describing how to treat the wound. "Sarah was a trooper—she's going to be fine."

Dave thanked the doctor. "Let's get out of here, honey. I'm taking you home."

Before they left, Sarah said, "Okay, now will someone tell me what just happened?"

The explanation fell to Nick, who told Sarah what little he saw. "I can't say for sure, but I locked eyes with this guy and had a bad feeling. I saw the pistol, but before I could process what was going on, the muskets fired, and he fired with them. I don't know who the guy was, but I did get a pretty good look at him. The detectives want me to look at some mug shots."

Realizing that Dave's car was still at Boone Hall, Allen got the keys and insisted on picking it up and driving it back. After locating the car, Allen drove it back to Dave and Sarah's place, with Nick following. Nick dropped Allen off at his condo and then headed back to Amy's apartment. It was after 6:00 p.m. by the time he got there.

"I don't know about you, babe," Amy said, "but I could use a glass of wine." Nick retrieved a bottle of chardonnay from the fridge and poured her a healthy glassful. He grabbed a Coke for himself, and they collapsed on the couch. Amy turned on the TV and flipped to the news. A pretty blond reporter stood at the entrance to Boone Hall, recounting what sparse details she'd been able to gather on the shooting. She didn't have many specifics, but she did report that one of the visitors had been grazed by a bullet. Sarah's name wasn't mentioned. They both listened intently until the reporter signed off.

"What'd you think, Nick? You didn't say much at the hospital."

"I know. I felt like anything I said would just make everyone more freaked than they already were."

"That makes sense." Amy switched off the TV. "It's just you and me now. So, any ideas?"

Nick thought for a moment. "Well, there's no way that guy was some random nutjob. He was a pro. He was definitely targeting one of us."

"Who do you think?"

"Well, I can't see any reason why it would be Dave or you. Had to be Allen, Sarah, or me."

"What do we do now," Amy quickly added, "stay inside and lay flat on the floor with the blinds shut?"

Nick lamented, "Well, maybe we don't have to be that extreme, but we do need to watch our backs. I'm sure Allen thinks it has something to do with the mob and his testimony. Sarah's a smart lady, and she's probably thinking the same thing. Allen told me he won't let her in the office without him being there. And when you start teaching, I'll stay here until you leave for class and try to be back by the time you get home. Josh, Zach, and Angela probably saw the news already, but I'll give them a call. I can also get ahold of my friends at the station and ask them to do drive-bys of Allen's office and Sarah's condo."

"All right," Amy said. "I've had enough excitement for one day." She slid closer to Nick. "How about we think of something else to do?" She started to unbutton his shirt and then paused and cocked her head, a sly smile emerging. "Got any ideas, Giordano?"

CHAPTER TWENTY-THREE

A DETECTIVE CALLED Nick early Sunday afternoon and asked him to come into the station to look at mug shots. Nick spent several hours going through police mug books with no luck. It seemed clear that the shooter was probably from outside the Charleston area.

While Nick was scrutinizing the mug books, Patsy Trantino and Jimmy Esposito were having a late lunch at The Belmont on King Street. Patsy was complaining about his wife when Jimmy interrupted him.

"Hey, Patsy. Hold on a sec. I wanna see this."

The television was broadcasting a follow-up report on the shooting at Boone Hall. The reporter was explaining that the Mt. Pleasant Police Department had confirmed that the spectator who had been shot was treated at MUSC and released.

Patsy laughed. "Civil War reenactment, my ass. Looks like those assholes were using real bullets!"

Esposito's eyes were still glued to the television. "Well, I gotta admit it takes balls to try to clip someone in broad daylight," Esposito muttered.

Patsy went back to bitching about his wife, but Jimmy Esposito was paying little attention. He was thinking about Carlo Tucci.

~~~

Ed Merchant was still in his office at 8:00 p.m. Sunday night when his cell rang. He recognized Jimmy Esposito's number and lowered his voice. "Yes."

"You alone?"

"Yeah. Go ahead."

"The thing at the plantation yesterday. I got something."

"Go ahead."

"Name's Carlo Tucci. Mobbed up out of New York City."

"Where is he?"

"Room 116. Best Western. Savannah Highway."

Jimmy Esposito disconnected the call, and the line went dead. Their mole in the mob had come through. Merchant thought for a moment and then picked up his desk phone and dialed Chito Walker.

The commander of Charleston's SWAT Team answered on the first ring, "SWAT Commander Walker." Merchant told Walker what he'd just learned. "Get your people mobilized for a 'high-risk person' strike. Strike time at zero hundred hours." Merchant passed on additional information concerning the
~~~

"high-risk person" strike, including who the target was and the assault location.

At 11:30 p.m. that night, Merchant rendezvoused with Walker and his twelve-man SWAT Team at the rear of Charleston Fire Station 11—less than a mile from the Best Western. The assault plan was reviewed and equipment double-checked. At 11:50 p.m., Walker gathered the team. "It's go time, let's move," he said. Then they left in two armored vehicles.

Two three-man teams secured the perimeter of the motel while Merchant, Walker, and the remaining officers inserted foam earplugs and approached room 116. The teams took their positions. One officer readied a fifty-pound battering ram. Commander Walker made a final visual check and signaled the officer with the ram to proceed.

The door was shattered on the first attempt. A flash bang grenade was pitched through the open door. The officers turned away, and two seconds later, a blinding flash of light and an intensely loud *bang* shook the room. The officers rushed in yelling, "Police! Police! Police!" and found Carlo Tucci on the floor, temporarily blinded and completely disoriented. Two officers held him down while he was cuffed. They dragged him out of the room and put him in the back of one of the vehicles. Six team members piled in behind Tucci, and the vehicle left for their main station on Lockwood Boulevard.

Commander Walker, Merchant, and the six remaining officers stayed at the Best Western, securing the premises for the follow-up investigation. The entire assault, from the time they arrived until Tucci was secured and in the armored vehicle, lasted less than ninety seconds.

CHAPTER TWENTY-FOUR

NICK WAS ASLEEP early Monday morning when his cellphone jarred him awake. "Hello," he answered groggily.

"Giordano, Ed Merchant here."

Nick saw the digital clock on the nightstand: 5:46 a.m. "Hang on," he whispered and rolled out of bed, careful not to wake Amy. He shut the bedroom door quietly behind him and flipped on the overhead light in the kitchen. There was now an anxious tone in his voice. "What's going on?"

"I need you down at Lockwood."

"When?"

"Now."

From the sound of Merchant's voice, Nick knew not to question him further. "All right, I'm on my way. Be there in fifteen minutes." Nick disconnected the call and returned to the bedroom. He pulled on a pair of pants, slipped on his shoes, and was about to rush out to his truck when he glanced at Amy, still fast asleep in bed. The moonlight filtered through the window throwing a soft silver light across her sleeping face. He didn't want to leave her alone. This situation was becoming increasingly chaotic, increasingly dangerous. If anything happened to her or any of his friends, he wouldn't be able to forgive himself. But now he couldn't do anything but leave. He scribbled a quick note and left it on the counter, barely resisting the urge to sign off with "Love, Nick."

Charleston's morning commute traffic hadn't kicked in yet, and he was across the James Island Connector in less than ten minutes, arriving at the station at 6:10 a.m.

He recognized the desk sergeant and said, "Frank, Ed Merchant wants to see me."

"Giordano, nice to see you again. Ed's in his office. I'll buzz you in."

Merchant's door was open, and as soon as he saw Nick, he stood up. "Come with me," he said.

Nick followed Ed down the hallway and entered a small room. Seeing the large one-way glass window, he knew exactly where he was. The only furniture in the room on the other side of the glass was a metal table and three metal chairs. Its walls and ceiling were painted a dingy white and lit by the harsh glare of two overhead florescent lights. In rooms like this, the goal is to keep the person being interrogated uncomfortable. Considering the intent, the room had achieved its goal.

Merchant pointed through the window. "Take a look at that guy. Tell me if you recognize him."

Nick took a step closer and stared at the man in the other room. His feet and left arm were cuffed to a chair; cigarettes, an ashtray, and a Styrofoam cup of coffee were on the table in front of him.

"How'd you find him?"

"You seen him before?"

"Yeah, he's the guy who shot Sarah at the reenactment. Who is he?" Merchant didn't answer. "I said who is he, Ed?"

"Are you positive he's the same man?"

"100 percent. Now, who is he?"

"He's a person of interest."

"Don't give me that shit, Ed. That son of a bitch tried to kill me!"

Merchant knew Nick would probably figure it out himself—or worse, go rogue—if he didn't give him something. "All right. This doesn't leave this room. Understand?"

"Yeah. You have my word."

Ed turned away from Nick and stared through the window at Carlo Tucci. "He's connected to the Genovese family out of New York City."

Nick felt a spark of excitement, as if a fog had lifted, as if the pieces of a puzzle had begun to fall into place.

"Son of a bitch. I knew this guy was a pro. But it's not like the mob to make a daytime hit in a crowded place. Those days are gone. Looks like they got a little impatient after all."

"Looks that way," Ed said. "I've talked to NYC's Organized Crime Unit and one of the U.S. attorneys who's prosecuting Rossini."

"Stanley Scott?" Nick questioned.

"Right. He's flying in later this morning. Now you know why none of this can get out. No one knows we've got him."

"I won't say a word," Nick quickly added. "What are you going to do with him?"

"With your testimony, we've got him on several counts of attempted murder. We'll obviously try to get him to flip on whoever ordered the hit."

"Good luck with that if he's a made man," Nick said.

"Maybe so, but the guy's got to be in his sixties. If we nail him, he'll spend the rest of his life in prison." Merchant put his arm on Nick's shoulder and led him from the room. "Listen Nick, we appreciate your help. And not a word to anyone."

"Understood," Nick replied. "But let me know what goes down with this, okay?"

"As much as I can."

It was after 6:30 a.m. by the time Nick left the station. He felt as if a weight had been lifted. With Carlo Tucci in custody, the threat from the mob was at least temporarily eased. But there was still Sullivan, Ivy, and the White Knights to deal with—not to mention the Beltrán-Leyva Cartel. The Coffee Cup was on his way back to James Island, and he stopped there to pick up coffee and muffins.

Amy was still sleeping when he got back to her apartment. He sat next to her on the bed for a moment, her long chestnut hair falling haphazardly on the white bedsheets. She looked serene, even fragile in her slumber—such a contrast to the worlds of Carlo Tucci, Mario Rossini, and Mason Ivy. He gently kissed her on the neck and whispered, "Wake up, Sleeping Beauty."

Amy opened her eyes and smiled. "What time is it?"

"After seven." Nick held up the coffee and muffins. "Breakfast is served."

"Aw, Nick, you're my Prince Charming. I could definitely get used to this."

With everything going on, Nick wanted to keep Amy close. "This is your last day before you start teaching. Why don't you come out to the Academy with me? You can hang out there, and I'll make it a short day. I'll take you to High Cotton for dinner." He chuckled. "It'll be like 'The Last Supper.'"

"I'd like that. Plus, it's been a while since I've seen Sally and the guys."

~~~

Later that morning, Ed Merchant and Stanley Scott sat in the interrogation room. They didn't say much—they were ready. And then an officer opened the door and Tucci shuffled in, his hands and ankles shackled. Once inside, an officer cuffed his left wrist to the arm of one of the chairs.

"Mr. Tucci, this is Mr. Scott. He'd like to have a few words with you."

Stanley Scott placed his briefcase on the table and fixed his attention on Carlo. "Good morning, Mr. Tucci." He turned to Merchant. "I'll take it from here." Ed left and settled into the
~~~

room on the other side of the glass, where he could watch and listen to the encounter.

Scott removed a tape recorder from his briefcase and placed it on the table. He also brought out a notepad and pen. He leaned forward, both elbows on the table, his fingers interlaced, and stared at Carlo for a few seconds before speaking. "First of all, I want to assure you that only a few people are aware we have you in custody. We'd like to keep it that way as long as possible. But you need to understand that we have a witness who has identified you as the shooter at the Civil War reenactment. One of the bullets you fired is with ballistics. We're confident it will be matched to the gun we retrieved from your hotel room.

"We are aware of your association with the Genovese family and that you have carried out several, shall we say, assignments for the family over the years. We're also concerned for the safety of your daughter, Sofia." Scott paused for a few seconds, watching his face closely, hoping it would reveal something. But Carlo's face remained motionless, like a high-stakes poker player.

Scott pushed. "We understand she lives with you in your Brooklyn Heights home on Claremont Avenue. I've been told Sofia gets on surprisingly well considering her medical affliction." This time, Carlo Tucci's face twitched at the sound of Sofia's name.

"You are now facing multiple aggravated attempted murder charges. Considering your background, each could carry a life sentence." He paused, a benevolent smile appearing on his face, and continued. "It is our hope we can work something out that would help both you and your daughter's situation." And then the smile vanished as quickly as it had come. "We both know your associates in New York wouldn't bat an eye at using your daughter to keep you quiet." Scott sat motionless, his dispassionate gaze fixed on Carlo.

Carlo returned a stare that could cut steel. He'd just been threatened, and he had no doubt the threat was real. He was going to prison. He could handle that. But what he couldn't handle was the thought of what the mob might do to Sofia. He closed his eyes, his mind flooded with images of his days on the docks and at the Fulton Fish Market. He remembered the face of Vincent "The Chin" Gigante the night he took the "oath of Omerta," when the Virgin Mary burned in his hands. The twisted faces of men he'd killed began to appear one after the other. They finally faded, replaced by the smiling face of Sofia.

Carlo opened his eyes and bowed his head. His shoulders slumped forward from the weight of a lifetime of regret. "What do you want?" he finally managed to ask.

"What can you give us, Carlo?"

Carlo raised his head. "I want my daughter here with me."

"That can be arranged."

"I want we should disappear. I want witness protection for both of us."

Scott paused before answering. "That could possibly be arranged. But you're asking a lot, Carlo. We'd need something of considerable value to even consider such a request. Considerable value, Carlo. Do you have something we might consider that valuable?"

"How can I trust you?"

"I am a U.S. attorney and have the authority to grant your requests. I give you my word that if what you provide is enough, you and your daughter will be protected."

"I'd need that in writing."

"That can be done. Now tell me, Carlo, what do you have?"

Tucci leaned forward. "I can give you Bellomo and Rossini. But I want my daughter here with me before I say another word."

"I'll see what I can do."

Scott stood and nodded toward the mirrored window. A moment later, Merchant and two uniformed officers entered the room. The officers removed the cuffs, and Tucci was taken away.

As soon as the door was shut, Merchant said, "Jesus Christ."

Scott withdrew his cell and made a call. He said, "Here's want I want you to do."

~~~

At 9:30 p.m. that evening, Tucci found himself back in the interrogation room. But this time, Carlo was not cuffed. He removed a cigarette and lit it. A few minutes later, Scott and Merchant entered.
~~~

Scott took a seat and nodded to Merchant, who slid a laptop computer in front of Carlo. He pressed a key and a video appeared showing Sofia standing between two men in front of the distinctive image of Charleston's Arthur Ravenel Jr. Bridge. Sofia began to sign. *Papa, are you all right? These men brought me here. They said you needed to see me.*

"I want her here with me," Tucci growled.

"You talk first," Scott replied and pushed the record button on the tape player. He identified himself and the date.

He continued, "I am in the Charleston, South Carolina Police Station located at 180 Lockwood Boulevard. Present in the room with me are Captain Edward Merchant and Mr. Carlo Tucci." Scott turned and looked directly at Carlo. "Mr. Tucci, please describe your association with a Mr. Liborio Bellomo and a Mr. Mario Rossini."

CHAPTER TWENTY-FIVE

NICK AND AMY spent most of Monday out at the Academy. Amy enjoyed a relaxing morning commiserating with Sally. Isaiah showed up about 1:00 p.m., and Amy spent the rest of the afternoon helping him with his chores and spending time with Josh and Zach.

Later that afternoon, Nick and Amy were in the office getting ready to leave. "Sally, we're gonna take off. Amy starts her student teaching tomorrow, and we're going to High Cotton to celebrate."

"You two go on and have fun tonight. I've got plenty to do here, and Isaiah can keep me company."

Sally gave Amy a hug and said, "You'll do great tomorrow, sweetheart. And come back soon. I'm the only lady around here, and it's tiresome being surrounded by all this testosterone!"

They had a nice meal at High Cotton, their conversation obviously centering on Amy's big day. She was understandably both excited and nervous. They had just settled in back at Amy's place when Nick's cell rang. He answered it with a hint of annoyance. "Hello." His irritation immediately turned to concern. "Yes, this is Mr. Giordano." He listened intently for the next twenty to thirty seconds and then said, "I'll be right there."

Amy could see the anxious look on his face. "What's the matter?"

"That was the Johns Island police. I need to get out to the Academy. Sally and Isaiah have been hurt."

"Oh God, what happened?"

"Not sure."

"I'm coming with you."

"No!" His voice left no room for further discussion. "I'll call you as soon as I know something." He was out the door before Amy could say another word.

It took less than twenty minutes for Nick to get to the Academy, breaking the speed limit and running a few red lights along the way. He was approaching the Academy when he saw several police cruisers and an EMS van parked in front of the office. He pulled into the lot and jumped out, leaving the truck's door open.

He approached the EMS van but was stopped by an officer.

"This is my place," Nick shouted and knifed past him to the open rear door of the van. Isaiah was lying there, an oxygen mask over his face, two paramedics working on him. There was blood everywhere. He was breathing but unconscious. The driver ushered Nick out of the way, shut the van's rear doors, and told the police officer they were taking Isaiah to MUSC Trauma Center.

Nick turned back and said, "Where's Sally?"

The officer waved for Nick to follow him. "She's inside. She's been hurt, but it doesn't look to be too bad."

Sally was sitting at her desk, a towel pressed to the side of her head.

"Jesus, Sally. What happened?" Nick asked.

"Mr. Giordano, right?" An officer standing next to Sally cut in. Nick nodded. "I'm Lieutenant Wallace. Three men entered the premises about an hour ago. They were armed and wore masks. Apparently, they were looking for you. Mrs. Reed here refused to tell them anything, and one of them struck her in the head with the butt of a gun. Mr. Robinson attempted to intercede but was severely beaten. He's been stabilized and will be taken to the hospital."

"Any idea who these people were?"

"No, not at this point. Mrs. Reed will need some stitches to close her head wound and will be checked for a concussion." At that moment, another officer entered and said they were ready to take Sally to the hospital.

"Give me a few minutes with her," Nick said.

"All right," Wallace agreed, "but make it quick."

Nick went to Sally, bent down, and took her hand. "I'm so sorry, Sally."

A stern look appeared on her face. "Not your fault, dear. I'll be fine. But I'm worried about Isaiah. Oh God, Nick. It was terrible what they did to that poor man."

Nick closed his eyes, trying to repress images of how awful that scene must have been. "Did you see any of the men?"

"No, they all wore Barack Obama masks, like the kind kids wear for Halloween."

"Anything else?"

"I did see them leave. The car was an old beat-up red one. Some sort of big truck or SUV."

"A Chevy Silverado?"

"Could've been. The license plate was covered with dirt, but I did see that the back was smashed up."

"Are you sure about that?"

"I saw what I saw."

"All right, Sally. They're going to take you to the hospital now. I'll be there later to make sure you get back home."

The officer walked Sally to his squad car, and they left for MUSC. Nick and Lieutenant Wallace were outside watching them leave when Nick asked, "So, what now?"

Wallace looked at Nick. "Ms. Reed told us you used to be a cop."

"Yeah, K-9 Unit. But that was years ago."

"Maybe so, but you know the drill. We'll need to check your security cameras and see what other evidence we can find here. Ms. Reed said they wore masks and gloves, so I'm not holding my breath. We'll be here another hour or two. Any ideas who might have reasons to do this?"

Nick thought for a second before answering. He'd promised Merchant not to divulge anything about Tucci or the White Knights. He didn't know if Sally had told them about the

Silverado but decided to leave that alone for the time being. "I was with the woman who was shot out at that Civil War reenactment on Saturday, and my apartment was broken into last week. I don't know who was behind either, but the Mt. Pleasant and Charleston police are investigating."

"We'll definitely follow up on that to see if there's any connection."

"I need to get to the hospital to check on Isaiah and Sally," Nick said.

Wallace nodded. "You can go, but I'll need to talk to you once we finish up here."

"Thanks, lieutenant. I'll have one of my people come out in an hour or so to lock up when you're finished. Please call me if you learn anything else."

On his way downtown, Nick called Josh and told him what had happened. Josh agreed to go to the Academy, check on the dogs, and make sure it was locked up once the police were done. Then he called Amy. She was obviously upset and wanted to meet Nick at the hospital. He convinced her to stay put—she needed her rest before her first day at school. He promised he'd call with any news on Isaiah and Sally.

It was almost 9:00 p.m. when Nick got to MUSC. He learned that Isaiah had already been treated and admitted. He'd sustained multiple cuts and lacerations on his face and head, a severe concussion, and a broken arm but no life-threatening injuries. An MRI revealed no evidence of cranial bleeding. Nick was allowed to look in on him, but he was heavily sedated.

Sally had received six stitches to close the cut above her left eye and was discharged shortly after Nick arrived. He drove her back to Johns Island. Sally insisted on Nick dropping her off at the Academy so she could get her car. A squad car had been assigned to keep an eye on her house. He made it to Amy's apartment shortly after 11:00 p.m. She was still up.

It took a while, but Nick assured Amy both Isaiah and Sally would be okay. They were both exhausted and asleep by 11:45 p.m.

~~~

For the second night in a row, Nick was awoken by his cell-phone. He fumbled for it and whispered, "What?"

"I need a good book to read." Then the line went dead. The digital clock read 3:30 a.m.

There was no traffic at that hour, and Nick was across the Connector and downtown in less than ten minutes. He continued up Calhoun, taking a left onto Ashley. A few hundred yards down Ashley, he slowed and pulled to the side of the road. He turned off the engine, killed the lights, and got out. Silence blanketed the city. It was like a ghost town. The dark buildings seemed asleep, the streetlights like nightlights. He walked up Ashley, the *squish, squish, squish* of his Nikes on pavement the only sound interrupting the stillness. He slowed when he saw the sign hanging lifeless in front of the bookshop.

"Over here," a voice emanated from the alcove next to Quarter Moon Books. Nick took a few paces toward the alley
~~~

and recognized Fitzpatrick huddled in a nest of shadows against the side of the building. He waved Nick closer.

"Are your people all right?"

"What?" Nick said.

"The people at your place. Were they hurt bad?"

Nick realized Terry was talking about Sally and Isaiah. He took a step closer to Fitzpatrick. "Did your people do this, Terry?"

"First of all, they're not 'my people.' But yes, the White Knights are behind this. Were they hurt bad?"

"Damn right they were hurt!" Nick caught himself and lowered his voice. "Both of them should be okay, though. I want names."

"Popeye Sullivan, Gus James, and Riley Plant. But that's not all. Sullivan's deep in the drug scene. He knows you were a cop and thinks you're still working undercover. Apparently, Sullivan got the go ahead from Mason Ivy."

"My apartment was tossed last week. Did Sullivan do that, too?"

"Don't know anything about that, but it wouldn't surprise me. Whatever the case, Sullivan wants to take you out. The White Knights have a deal with Beltrán's people. They'll be making their move on the drug market soon. I don't know when precisely. But it's coming."

"Does Merchant know all this shit?"

"Yeah, he knows. Listen, that's all I got. I'm sorry about your people. Just watch yourself. All hell's gonna break loose when this thing goes down." Then Fitzpatrick disappeared around the corner of the bookstore.

Nick headed back to his truck. He'd already figured out that whoever hit the Academy were the same people who shot up Union Baptist. The damaged red Silverado tied the two attacks together. And Fitzpatrick had just confirmed that Sullivan and his boys were behind both those attacks. It was also clear that Mason Ivy's White Knights were tied to the Beltrán-Leyva Cartel and were about to move on Charleston's drug trade.

CHAPTER TWENTY-SIX

WHILE AMY WAS getting dressed, Nick made a quick breakfast.

She joined him in the kitchen. "Well, how do I look?"

"Well educated," Nick smiled. "And stunningly good looking."

"I'm a little nervous. I didn't get much sleep. Couldn't stop thinking about Sally and Isaiah. Nick, I'm really scared. Those church attacks, Sarah getting shot, and everything else that's been happening."

"I know, babe. It's been crazy. Listen, I'm supposed to talk to the police again today. They'll figure all this out. I don't want you to worry. Just focus on your school today. Promise?"

"I promise," Amy answered and then noticed the time. "It's almost 6:30. I gotta run."

Nick gave her a quick kiss and handed her a piece of toast. "Here, eat this on the way. You'll do great."

It felt strange to Nick to go to work as if it was just another day, when he was, in fact, returning to a crime scene. But someone still had to take care of the dogs—he had a business to run.

Nick pulled into the Academy and was surprised to see Sally's car parked in the lot. Nick shut off the engine and remained seated in his truck for a moment. He felt humbled by Sally's dedication and how much Josh, Zach, and Isaiah had given of themselves to him and his company. He felt guilty he was involved in bringing all this danger down on them. He thought of Angela and Sarah Pryor and her husband, Dave. They had nothing to do with this shit, but they'd all been drawn into it.

He got out of the truck thinking to himself, *Well, at least they've got Tucci, and Merchant knows about Sullivan and the White Knights. Maybe this whole thing will end soon.*

He walked into the office, and Sally was at her desk. "Sally, what in the world are you doing here? You should be home resting."

"Pshaw! I'm fine, plus someone's gotta keep this place running." She pulled open her desk drawer and removed a small Sig Sauer P238 handgun.

"Christ, Sally, where did you get that thing?"

She returned the gun to her drawer. "Nick, don't forget I worked for the Johns Island Police Department for twenty-five years. I've had this little puppy for years."

He was furious with himself. Now his employees were carrying guns around with them for protection. "Just keep that thing locked in the drawer! Where's Josh?"

"He was in first thing this morning and left for Atlanta to drop off Trooper and Rusty. He won't be back 'til later this evening."

When Nick walked into his office, he was somewhat surprised to see Zach seated in a chair next to his desk. "Morning, Zach. Josh won't be back from Atlanta until tonight. So go ahead and get started with your dogs. I'll be out in a minute to help."

Nick sat down and was removing some papers from his briefcase when he realized that Zach hadn't moved. He gave him a questioning look. "What's up?"

Zach held up a photo of Popeye Sullivan and another man leaning against the back of a red Chevy Silverado with a dented rear fender.

Zach pointed to the photo. "Who are these guys?"

"Where'd you get that?"

"On your desk. Who are they?" Nick explained that Allen had found the photo on the Internet. Zach's expression didn't change. "I said who are they?"

"Josh and I ran into one of the guys at that bar in Goose Creek. Why?"

Zach pointed at the Silverado in the photo. "Saw that car leavin' the church after Angela's mom got shot."

"Jesus, Zach. You sure?"

"What'd I just say?"

"All right. If you're positive about the Silverado, I need to get this to someone I know downtown." Nick purposely didn't mention that one of the guys in the photo was Tom Sullivan or that he had the addresses of his house in Summerville and his Goose Creek moving company.

"Listen, Zach. I'm gonna call Ed Merchant and let him know the guys in the photo with the Silverado were probably involved in the church shooting. We'll get these guys. I promise. I just don't want you doing anything that could mess it up."

Zach stood and left the room without saying another word. It was obvious he didn't have the same relationship of trust with the police that Nick did. And Nick was concerned he might not choose to wait for the police to move on Sullivan.

Nick called Merchant and told him what he'd just learned. Ed had answered in a foul mood, but his curiosity spiked several notches when he heard the news connecting Sullivan to the church shooting.

"I need that photo. When can you get down here?"

"I'll be right there."

Nick made it to Narcotic/Vice and was led back to Ed's office.

"Shut it," Merchant said. Nick shut the door, approached Merchant, and slid a copy of the photo across his desk.

"The guy on the right is Tom Sullivan. Allen copied the photo from Sullivan's Facebook page. Josh and I ran into him out at the Iron Horse last week. My guy, Zach Brown, swears the Silverado in the photo is the same one he saw leaving Union Baptist right after the shooting."

Merchant was well aware of who Tom Sullivan was, but connecting him to the Silverado and Union Baptist shooting was new. "All right," Ed said. "We'll take it from here."

"Okay, but there's also a chance he's the one who tossed my apartment. The detectives working the case are going to look at my building's security footage. They've got a copy of the photo, so you need to check with them."

Ed stood. "Make sure your guy, Zach Brown, stays away from this."

"I'll do what I can, but I can't watch him 24/7. Just keep me in the loop, okay?"

Merchant didn't react to Nick's request. "Now get out of here so I can move on this." Nick was leaving when Ed said, "Hey, Giordano, you did good." Nick smiled, somewhat surprised at Ed's last comment. Like most cops, not much usually got through Merchant's emotional armor.

When Nick got back to the Academy, he noticed that Zach's truck was gone. He asked Sally where Zach went. "He told me he had some errands to run and would be back this afternoon."

~~~

The hospital called an hour later advising Nick that Isaiah was ready to be discharged. The doctor met Nick outside Isaiah's hospital room and explained the extent of his injuries and what
~~~

needed to be done during his recovery. His right arm had sustained a compound fracture, four ribs were broken, and his face had required about thirty stitches to close its wounds. Arrangements had been made to move Isaiah to a local senior living facility, where he could be taken care of during his recovery.

When Nick entered his hospital room, Isaiah was dressed and seated in a wheelchair. His right arm was casted and in a sling. Nick stopped dead when he saw Isaiah's face—it was severely swollen and almost completely covered with bandages and gauze. Despite his condition, sparks of his cantankerous personality emerged when he told Nick how he'd almost had those "sons-a-bitches."

Lieutenant Wallace had stopped by the hospital that morning to interview Isaiah, but he was unable to provide much insight into what happened.

After Nick got Isaiah admitted and settled in the assisted living facility, he met Amy at her school so she could show him her new classroom. He managed to keep his emotions under control despite the frustration and anger building inside him. On his way to Amy's apartment, he called Sally to check on Zach. He was alarmed to learn that Zach had never made it back to the Academy that afternoon.

Back at her apartment, Amy was describing everything that happened that day at the school and how excited the kids were to meet their new teacher. He was half listening to her recount her meeting with the principal when he sat bolt upright and said, "Oh shit!"

Amy froze mid-sentence. "Geez, Nick. What is it?"

Nick quickly composed himself. "Sorry, Amy. I just remembered I needed to call Josh. I'll be right back."

He ducked outside and called Josh. He was on his way back from Atlanta and told Nick he should get in town around 8:30 p.m. "Okay, I need you to go straight to the Academy. I'll meet you there. I'll explain everything when I see you tonight."

Josh was obviously curious. But hearing the anxious tone in Nick's voice, he knew not to push it. "I'll be there."

Nick felt like kicking himself. How could he be so foolish. He couldn't believe he'd forgotten that Allen had written the addresses of Tom Sullivan's house in Summerville and his moving company in Goose Creek on the back of the photo of Sullivan and the Silverado. And he wasn't naïve enough to think Zach hadn't seen those addresses. Zach may not have known the guy in the photo was Tom Sullivan, but now he sure as hell knew where he could find him.

~~~

At about 8:00 p.m. that evening, Nick told Amy he needed to drive out to the Academy and finish up some things he didn't get to that afternoon. "Don't know how long I'll be, but don't wait up for me. You didn't get much sleep last night. Plus, it's rise and shine at 5:45."

Nick got to the Academy at 8:30 p.m. Josh arrived about fifteen minutes later. "All right, boss," Josh said, "let's have it. What's up?"
~~~

Nick showed Josh the photo of Sullivan next to the Silverado and explained that Zach had identified the Silverado in the photo and figured out Sullivan was behind both the church and Academy attacks. He turned the photo over and pointed to the two addresses. "You gotta figure Zach saw those addresses.

"He left the Academy this morning and never came back. Now that he's got those addresses, I'm afraid he's going to do something crazy. Here's what I want to do. We've got no real proof of what Sullivan and his buddies did, either here or at the church. I figure we go out there tonight and sit on Sullivan's place. If Zach shows up, we can stop him. Also, we might learn something that'll push the cops to act."

"So, what if this Sullivan guy makes us?" Josh asked.

"He makes us, we let him go," Nick said. "Nobody gets hurt. We don't want a repeat of what happened at Westcott."

Josh nodded. "I can't believe we're doing this shit again."

"Yeah, but no guns this time. I got a better idea. Wait here." Nick jogged to the kennels and a minute later returned with Nitro, a ninety-pound German Shepherd.

Nitro hopped into the back seat, and Nick slid into the front. Josh pulled out of the Academy, and they settled in for the thirty-five-minute drive to Summerville. Neither said much—each lost in his own thoughts anticipating what might happen. As they approached Exit 199 off I-26, Nick punched Sullivan's address into his phone and told Josh to take the exit and follow North Main for about six miles.

Ten minutes later, they turned left onto Gants Road. "All right, pull up over here and shut off your lights." Josh did, and Nick pointed to the car next to a small single-story house. "There's the Silverado."

They settled in to wait, eyes focused on the house and the Silverado. A few moments later, Josh said, "I still don't get it, Nick. You said the cops know about this Popeye Sullivan guy and the White Knights Klan group. Plus, they were at your apartment after it got trashed. And then there's what happened last night at the Academy. Hell, they know about all those church attacks, too. Why haven't they done something?"

"I don't know, Josh. Like I said, maybe they don't think they've got enough. Maybe they think they'll blow the whole thing if they move too soon. And the FBI's wrapped up in this, too. I know they're investigating the mob and the church shooting. You know how the cops and the Feds feel about each other. Protecting their turf and all that."

Nick was about to say something else when he noticed two men leave the house and head to the Silverado. Nick whispered, "All right, Josh. Follow them."

The Silverado backed out of the driveway and headed toward the Dodge. They ducked low in their seats until the Silverado had passed and was well down the road. Josh made a U-turn and headed after them, remaining several hundred yards behind. They followed the Silverado for more than fifteen miles out of Summerville and into Goose Creek until it turned onto Red Bank Road.

The undergrowth on either side of the road was thick with wax myrtle, bayberry, and yaupon holly, and what few houses they saw were mobile homes. About a mile down Red Bank, Sullivan turned into a gravel parking lot in front of a small prefab steel building surrounded by thick woods. The sign on the building read, "Good Guys Moving." Three cars were parked in the lot.

Josh quickly pulled his truck behind a line of thick undergrowth out of sight of the building. The air was devoid of even a breath of breeze, and a faint mist hung low to the ground. "So, what now?" he asked.

Nick didn't answer. He remembered Fitzpatrick telling him that Popeye Sullivan was heavy into the illicit drug business. And Allen's computer work uncovered the fact that he owned a small moving company. Nick couldn't believe he hadn't put the two together. The moving company made the perfect front to move the cartel's drugs.

Nick pulled out his cell and called Ed Merchant's cell number. It rang four times and went to voicemail. The tension in Nick's voice was clear. "Ed, this is Nick Giordano. Call me back as soon as you get this!"

"Christ, Nick. Where's your buddy now?" Josh asked, frustration evident in the tone of his voice.

Nick checked his watch. It was almost 11:00 p.m. "We're gonna wait to hear from Merchant."

Josh shook his head—the scene felt too much like what had happened a few months ago out at the Westcott warehouse. "This is déjà vu all over again," he said.

An uncomfortable silence descended on them as the minutes dragged by. Finally, Josh turned to Nick. "Call him again." Nick tried Merchant's cell again—it again went to voicemail. "Christ, Nick. Call 911!"

"No," Nick answered, his voice a bit testy. "Zach's not here, so let's just leave. I'll keep trying Merchant."

Just as Josh was backing the truck up, Nick noticed a dark shape moving low to the ground through the mist toward the building. "Josh, wait." Nick pointed into the darkness. "Look over there!"

The figure quickly covered the fifty yards to the building—pressing himself up against the metal siding as he peered through the window. The ambient light from inside the building illuminated the sweat-covered, shaved black head of Zach Brown.

"Shit, Josh. That's Zach!"

The interior of the building was dimly lit and strewn with moving equipment. A good-sized box truck and an old forklift were parked near the rear of the place.

Eight men, four on each side, faced each other across a long folding table. Mason Ivy was on one side flanked by Popeye Sullivan and two other men. Everyone was armed—handguns stuck in belts, AK-47s slung over shoulders. The men facing Ivy and his crew were obviously Mexican cartel.

An open briefcase lay on the table next to what must have been twenty bricks of heroin. A short, heavyset Mexican, obviously the boss man, stepped forward and made a gesture toward the heroin. Popeye opened his switchblade, cut into one of the bricks, and tasted a sample of the white powder. The bitter taste of the product confirmed it was high purity heroin. He smiled and said something to Ivy.

Zach was concentrating on the group inside the building when he felt something hard and cold touch his left temple.

"*No te muevas hijo de puta*," a voice whispered. He felt a hand remove the revolver he'd stuffed in the back of his pants. The man holding the gun was huge—easily matching Zach's height and weight.

With the gun still pressed against Zach's head, the man grabbed him by the back of his neck and pushed him to the rear of the building. As he shoved him through the back door, he brought the butt of his gun down viciously on the nape of Zach's neck. He stumbled forward but surprisingly managed to stay upright. All eyes turned in his direction. Men on both sides of the table drew their guns.

There was a moment of confusion, everyone unsure what was happening. The short, heavyset man frowned and, in a heavy Mexican accent, asked who this man was. His eyes were dark and impenetrable—cold and flat like those of a predator.

Mason Ivy held up his hands. "How the hell do I know, Miguel? He's not one of ours."

Nick and Josh were now crouched by the side of the truck. From their vantage point, they had seen the man approach Josh but could do nothing. Nick held Nitro's control leash firmly in his left hand. Josh had removed his Beretta from his truck's lockbox and held it in his right hand.

Nick was about to start after Zach when a large hand grabbed his shoulder and kept him crouched. Nick swung his head around, his eyes falling on a helmeted man dressed in full body armor. The man's face was blackened with grease paint.

"Stand down," the man said. It was Ed Merchant. Next to him stood Chito Walker. Walker raised his left hand and waved it in a circular motion—signaling his men to deploy around the perimeter. The SWAT Team members were barely visible in their black body armor as they moved low to the ground toward the building. Merchant repeated his order for Nick to stay put and then quickly followed after his men.

By this time, Josh had already left and was headed towards the rear of the building.

"Aw, shit!" Nick muttered as he crouched down low to the ground and followed Josh—Nitro by his side.

Meanwhile, inside the building, both groups faced off, Zach's sudden appearance heightening their mutual skepticism and distrust. Ivy ordered his men to level their weapons on Zach. The Mexicans, their confusion mounting, began swinging their guns back and forth between Zach and Ivy's men.

Popeye leveled his handgun at the back of Zach's head. The man who'd brought Josh into the building quickly backed away.

"Bad move, tough guy," Popeye barked, cocking his gun. "Kiss your ass goodbye, motherfucker!"

A sharp crack echoed off the steel walls, and Popeye Sullivan's head exploded in a cloud of scarlet mist. Zach hit the floor as a hail of gunfire erupted, and SWAT team members poured into the building. Ivy lunged forward, grabbed the briefcase, and dove sideways, managing to roll behind the fork-lift. While bullets continued to fly, Ivy ran around the back of the box truck and through the rear exit. Holding the briefcase close to his chest, he made a beeline for the woods behind the building.

Nick and Josh were about twenty yards away when they saw Ivy burst through the door.

Nick snapped off Nitro's control collar and yelled, "Attack!"

Nitro was a blur as he bounded forward. He closed the distance in seconds, leapt, and buried his teeth into the back of Ivy's right thigh, driving him into the ground. The briefcase flew into the air and skidded across the dew-covered grass.

As if on cue, the gunfire suddenly stopped. All four of the cartel's men and two White Knights had been shot and were lying splayed out on the concrete. Zach was face first on the floor, hands still covering his head. Two SWAT members had been hit, but their chest armor had absorbed the force of the bullets. An acrid and sour smell hung inside the building as the officers surveyed the scene and began attending to the wounded.

Nick called off Nitro and stood a few feet from Ivy, who cradled his mangled leg. Nitro panted and stared intently at Ivy.

Just then, Ivy rolled over and tried to get up. Nick watched Josh's right leg fly forward, his Army boot connecting square on the center of Ivy's chest. "You ain't goin' nowhere, pecker-head!" roared Josh. Nick smiled, secretly hoping a few of Ivy's ribs were broken.

Josh and Nitro remained with Ivy, and Nick jogged to the building. He was met at the back door by Merchant. "Jesus, Ed, how did you find out all this was going down tonight? I only called about twenty minutes ago."

Merchant frowned. "Did you now? Well, I've been a little busy. We've been surveilling Ivy and his boys for some time. Plus, we got a heads up that one of Hector Beltrán's lieutenants by the name of Miguel Ramos entered the U.S. about a week ago and was sighted in Charleston. We put two and two together—we're actually pretty good at math. Now you've got some explaining to do, Giordano. What the hell are you doing out here? You and your boys almost ruined everything."

Before Nick could answer, he saw that two officers had Zach face down on the floor and were starting to cuff him. He told Merchant he was one of his guys, and Ed ordered his men to let him go. Nick pointed behind him to where Ivy was sprawled on the ground next to Josh and Nitro. Attempting to assuage Merchant's anger, he said, "He was trying to get away with a briefcase, probably full of cash. If we weren't here, he'd still be running through the woods." Merchant dispatched two officers to take care of Ivy and the drug money.

By that time, Zach, clutching the back of his neck, had joined Nick and Ed. Nick introduced the two men.

Ed, obviously still pissed at Nick, turned to him and said, "So, let's have it. We had this planned for days, and you almost blew up the whole thing."

Nick did his best to explain what he'd learned and how they'd followed Popeye Sullivan. He didn't mention the fact that Zach had tried to take things into his own hands. Finally, he gave Ed a sheepish grin and finished by saying, "Well, at least I tried to call you, Ed."

Merchant ordered two of his officers to secure the bricks of heroin and the drug money. Two SWAT vehicles and an EMS van pulled up to the building, and the paramedics began to treat the wounded. Several police and DEA agents arrived on the scene, and soon the place was crawling with uniformed and plainclothes personnel.

It was well after 2:00 a.m. before Nick, Josh, and Zach were permitted to leave. Nick and Josh walked Zach to his truck, which had been parked a few hundred feet up the road behind thick undergrowth. Josh said, "Well, that reminded me of a firefight in Afghanistan." Zach grunted his agreement.

Nick made it clear to Zach how disappointed he was that he'd taken off on his own. "That's the last time I want to see any shit like that. You got a problem in the future, we'll handle it together." Zach simply nodded and, as usual, said nothing.

Forty minutes later, Josh pulled up to Amy's apartment. Nick sat there for a minute before getting out. He was overwhelmed, relieved. He wanted to voice something profound, but the words eluded him. "I don't know what to say."

Josh put his hand on Nick's shoulder. "Nothing to say. Get some sleep, and I'll pick you up in the morning."

For the second night in a row, Nick quietly slipped into bed next to Amy, sound asleep, completely unaware of the events that had just transpired. Nick kissed her gently, laid back in bed, and eventually fell into a peaceful sleep.

CHAPTER TWENTY-SEVEN

THE EXCITEMENT OF the past few weeks soon waned, and a welcome routine slowly began to return to the Academy.

Isaiah was recovering nicely. Sarah picked him up a few times a week and took him to the Academy so he could make sure Nick and the guys were taking good care of the kennels and his precious dogs.

Allen, Angela, Sarah, and Dave joined Nick and his crew out at the Academy for Nick's annual Christmas party. Steve Williams, Ed Merchant, and their wives stopped by the party to share in the holiday cheer.

Sidney Scott flew into Charleston in late January to interview Nick, Josh, and Zach concerning what they'd witnessed the night of the raid on Popeye Sullivan's moving company. All three would eventually be called on to testify against Mason Ivy and Miguel Ramos at their drug trafficking and attempted murder trials.

Months passed, and the weather began to change. Soon the warm southern breezes of spring once again returned to grace the Lowcountry.

Amy completed her student teaching assignment with flying colors and was thrilled when her principal offered her a full-time teaching position at the school starting in the fall.

Amy had just donned her graduation gown and cap and was preparing to receive her degree in elementary education. The crowd gathered in the College of Charleston's Cistern Yard in front of Randolph Hall to watch the event. Amy's mom and sister, Cora, joined Nick as they watched Amy walk across the stage and proudly accept her diploma.

~~~

Some 750 miles away in New York City, Carlo Tucci was being escorted into the United States Federal Court for the Southern District of New York by four armed U.S. marshals. Carlo was there to testify in the racketeering and murder trials of Liborio Bellomo and Mario Rossini.

After completing his testimony, the marshals hustled Carlo to the rear of the courthouse, where a nondescript black van waited. Carlo and the marshals entered the van. It exited the alley, turned left onto Pearl Street, and disappeared into New York City's rush-hour traffic.

~~~

Spring was well underway when Mrs. Edna Swanson was at Tellmann's Market in New Salem, North Dakota, shopping for her annual Memorial Day cookout.

She'd just picked up several packages of ground sirloin from the butcher and was checking the next item on her shopping list. She looked up at the old butcher and said, "Excuse me, dear, now where in the world did they put the pickles?"

He returned her smiled and answered, "Let me see. I think they'd be on Aisle 12, Mrs. Swanson." He pointed to a young woman stacking cases of soda and added, "See the girl over there. She'd be happy to help you." The old man waved at the young lady. *Pickles?* he signed. She responded with a thumbs-up.

The old man smiled at the young lady. He was happier than he'd been in a long time, perhaps his whole life. *I love you*, he signed.

The young lady signed back, *I love you too, Papa.*

Another Nick Giordano Novel
Coming in 2018

SHARK BAIT

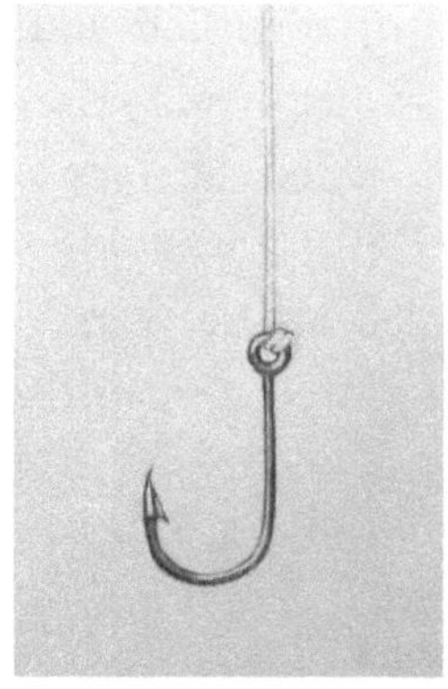

CHAPTER ONE

IT WAS THAT in-between time—a quiet stillness cradled the city. Its streets were empty with the exception of a random car or two passing beneath the soft orange glow of the street-lamps. The Holy City was at peace, as if enjoying its final hour before the faint whisper of gray appeared in the east ushering in the promise of a new day.

Allen Miller slipped on his Nike running shoes and took the elevator down from his sixth-floor Bee Street condo. It was approaching 5:00 a.m., and the city was shrouded in darkness as he headed north up Lockwood Drive past the RiverDogs baseball stadium. He glanced at his Apple Watch and picked up his pace. About twenty-five minutes later, he made a right off East Bay onto Calhoun Street, starting mile number four of his six-mile run through the streets of downtown Charleston, South Carolina.

These predawn runs helped him clear his mind and organize his day. This was his therapy—his outlet for shedding the sedentary ten-hour-day sessions sitting behind the computers at his cybersecurity company. The early morning air was crisp and clear. There was only a breath of breeze sliding off the waters of the Ashley River as he passed a small park at the corner of Calhoun and Rutledge.

A native of Charleston, Allen was an only child and enjoyed what might be called a privileged upbringing. His father, Julius, had just retired from his position as senior vice president of J.P. Morgan, where he headed up the company's investment banking business in Charleston. After his retirement, Julius continued to sit on several corporate boards and remain intimately connected to both Charleston's business and political scene. His wife, Elizabeth, also served on a number of boards at the heart of the city's social landscape. The Miller family had for generations been an important part of the so-called Charleston Elite.

From a young age, Allen showed a unique proclivity for computers and technology. His prowess in this area quickly surpassed the ability of his technology teachers at the Charleston Collegiate School to challenge him—so much so that he was invited to take advanced computer classes at the College of Charleston. After earning both undergraduate and graduate degrees in computer engineering and cybersecurity at the Massachusetts Institute of Technology (MIT), he joined the Department of Homeland Security's United States Computer Emergency Readiness Team (US-CERT). US-CERT is an elite team of computer professionals whose job it is to protect our nation's Internet infrastructure by coordinating defenses against and responses to cyberattacks.

Allen had a highly successful career at Homeland Security before leaving the government to start his own cybersecurity company, CyberNet Security Inc. After five years of working for someone else, he liked the idea of answering to nobody but himself. He operated out of a small second-floor office on Queen Street in downtown Charleston. Allen's reputation followed him to Charleston, and his company had little problem attracting a healthy number of corporate and individual clients.

Allen was beginning to settle into that floaty, free-form sense of well-being that his runs offered him when he caught a glimpse of a dark shape lying under a row of bushes in the rear of the park. Feeling a faint flicker of curiosity, he slowed and veered to his left. As he approached the line of bushes, it became apparent that the object in front of him was a body.

Allen thought to himself, *Probably some poor homeless guy sleeping it off.* But before the thought left his mind, his eyes fell on what was left of the man's face, leaving no doubt he was dead. The body was shirtless, and a number of deep gashes covered most of his face and shoulders. A closer look revealed that the side of his face was caved in like a smashed pumpkin, and his left eye socket was completely collapsed. Ligature marks had cut deep into his neck. Allen stumbled backwards when he saw that both of the man's hands were missing.

All of Allen's attention was focused on the dead man, and he took no notice of the hooded man getting into the black Ford van parked a hundred feet or so up Rutledge. The sound of the van accelerating drew Allen's attention, and he caught a few of the letters on its light-blue South Carolina license plate.

The van quickly disappeared down Rutledge into the dark grays of dawn. Allen immediately pressed the side button on his Apple Watch, automatically connecting him to a 911 operator. He reported where he was and what he'd just seen. The operator informed him that officers were being dispatched to the scene and instructed him to stay where he was and remain on the line. He then looked around the area. It was deserted—the black van nowhere to be found.

Two police officers arrived within minutes and, after confirming the victim was deceased, radioed their initial report to headquarters. One of the officers began to secure the area with bright-yellow crime scene tape—cordoning off a fairly large area around the body.

The other officer approached Allen. "You the guy who called this in?"

"Yes, sir."

The officer removed a small notepad. "What's your name?" Allen answered, and the officer continued. "So, tell me what you saw."

"Not much to tell, officer." Allen pointed at the body. "I was on my morning run and saw the body. When I got close enough, it was obvious the guy was dead, and I called 911."

"Did you see anyone else in the immediate area?"

"No."

After recording his name, address, and phone number and asking a few more general questions, the officer pointed to a bench a few feet away from where they were standing. "All right, Mr. Miller, you stay put. Detectives should be here shortly. They'll take it from here." The officer flipped his notepad closed. By this time, a few more police officers had arrived, and two plainclothes detectives were approaching the crime scene tape. The officer nodded toward the detectives. "There they are now."

The shorter of the two detectives took a final drag off his cigarette and flicked the butt behind him as he lifted the crime scene tape. He reminded Allen of Peter Falk's character in the old *Columbo* TV series. He gauged his age to be early to mid-fifties. His dark suit jacket and pants looked like they'd been slept in, and his longish gray/black hair was disheveled. The man's eyes seemed tired, and his dark, stubbled face was in dire need of a shave. He was followed under the tape by his much younger partner, who was clad in a dark-blue windbreaker and an open-collared white shirt. A gold detective shield was clipped to his designer jeans.

The officer standing with Allen again told him to stay where he was and headed over to join the other police officers and the two detectives. It was clear to Allen that the older, dark-suited detective was in charge. He questioned the officers for a moment or two until one of them pointed toward Allen. The dark suit issued a few more directions to the group and headed toward Allen. The windbreaker made his way to the dead body.

It was growing lighter now, and the city was beginning to stir. A small crowd had already gathered—curious about the bizarre scene and what was happening. Allen felt a wave of nausea as the enormity of what he'd just witnessed began to settle in: *What the hell did I just walk into?*

"Mr. Miller, I'm Detective Otto Klecker. I understand you discovered the body."

"Yes, sir."

Klecker glanced at Allen's outfit. "You run here often?"

"Maybe a few times a week. It's one of the routes I use."

The detective tilted his head slightly and asked, "What kind of work do you do?"

"I've got a small computer company." Allen pointed behind him. "My office is over on Queen close to East Bay."

The detective looked Allen up and down. A trace of a smile appeared and he said, "You the Allen Miller that was involved with that Mercy Hospital thing last year?"

"Yes, sir. That would be me."

Over a year ago, Allen had been hired by the CEO of a large Chicago-based corporation that owned Charleston's Mercy General Hospital. Narcotics seemed to be disappearing from the hospital. Allen was directed to use his exceptional computer expertise to covertly hack into Mercy's computer system in an effort to discover if this was, in fact, happening. Allen, along with his assistant, Sarah Pryor, uncovered how the drugs were being taken and who was behind the theft. His discovery led to a much larger criminal organization involved in drug trafficking, loansharking, prostitution, and money laundering. Allen was kidnapped and almost lost his life at the hands of the mob's Charleston boss, Max DiMarco, and his thugs. If it hadn't been for his friend Nick Giordano, Allen wouldn't be alive today.

"All right then," Klecker said, "I'm going to need to take your statement, but I've got a few things to do around here first. One of the officers will take you back to the station. I'll be there shortly. Shouldn't take more than an hour or so."

Detective Klecker headed back to his partner, who was in the process of taking pictures of the body and surrounding area. Another officer escorted Allen to his squad car. They were leaving for the police station when the CSI van arrived.

It was almost 7:00 a.m. by the time Allen arrived at the Lockwood Drive police station. He was put in an interrogation room and told to wait. A bit over an hour later, Otto Klecker entered the room and took a seat across from Allen.

He put a tape recorder and notebook in front of him. "You want some coffee or something?"

"No, sir. I'm good."

"All right then. Let's get started." The detective punched the player's record button, identified himself, the time and date, and began the interview. "I'm at the police station located at 180 Lockwood Drive, Charleston, South Carolina. With me in the room is Mr. Allen Miller." He nodded at Allen. "Mr. Miller, please tell me what happened this morning."

Allen recapped his morning from the time he awoke at 4:30 a.m. to when he arrived at the police station. Detective Klecker had a series of additional questions, which Allen answered. The interview concluded an hour later at 9:00 a.m.

Otto turned off the recorder, stood, and said, "Thank you, Mr. Miller. I'll have one of our officers drive you home."

"That won't be necessary," Allen answered. "It's only a half mile to my condo."

They left the interrogation room and walked down the hall to the reception area. Klecker shook Allen's hand and said, "All right. Thanks again. I'm sure I'll need to talk with you again."

Allen left the station, jogged the half mile up Lockwood, and was back inside his condo by 9:30 a.m. He showered, dressed, and headed to his office thirty minutes later.

ABOUT THE AUTHOR

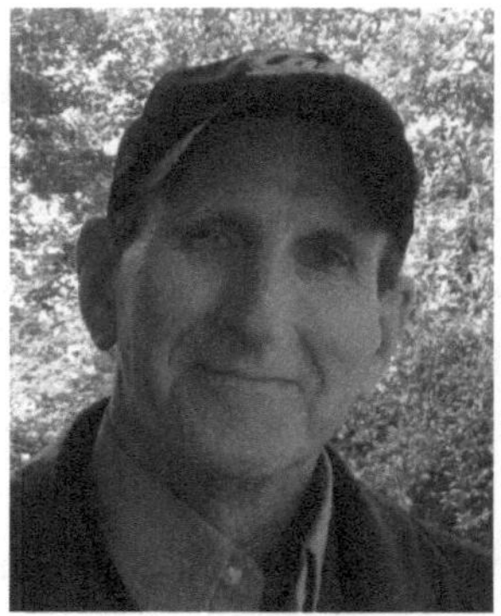

Geoff Collins holds graduate degrees in business and finance and a master's degree in education. He has held multiple management positions in Fortune 500 companies and was CEO of a Midwest advertising and public relations firm.

After a successful career in business, he taught elementary school for fifteen years. His passion for teaching reading and writing to his students led to a career as an author of both children stories and adult mysteries.

Geoff lives on Johns Island, South Carolina, with his wife, Sally. He has three grown children, Max, Leigh, and KC, and four grandchildren, John, Collin, Cora, and Lily.

OTHER BOOKS BY
GEOFF AND ART COLLINS

NIKKI AND THE TREE KEEPER

 *"What a wonderful and lovely tale!"*

 *"Nikki is a heart-warming and inspirational story of finding your place in the world."*

⭐⭐⭐⭐⭐ *"Nikki and the Tree Keeper is magical."*

⭐⭐⭐⭐⭐ *"The illustrations are beautiful and add so much to the book."*

www.booksbycollins.com

THE CHRISTMAS TOKEN

 *"The Christmas Token is a heart-warming holiday tale about generosity, memories, and family."*

 *"The artwork in this tender story is superior!"*

"The Christmas Token should become a family tradition to read as the Christmas season begins!"

"Excellent!"

"Lovely book! My kids have read it many times over the holidays."

www.booksbycollins.com

THE ADVENTURES OF ARCHIBALD
& JOCKABEB

 **"One of a kind!"**
This is the best book EVER!!!!!! Dragons, Indians, horses, evil crows, there is nothing like it! I loved it…can't wait for more adventures to come.

 **"A majestic tale—Harry Potter meets The Indian in the Cupboard"**
Loved reading these books. I quickly got hooked, dug in, and engaged with the characters. Wonderful stories."

 **"Rich in vocabulary!"**
This book is rich in vocabulary. I can't wait to read all the other Archibald and Jockabeb books!

 **"Best of the best!"**
In the Forest is an outstanding book! The characters are great and help make the wonderful story come together.

 **"Terrific series of action books!"**

www.theajadventures.com

WHITE CLOUD AND THE GOLDEN CANYON

 *Excellent Native American tale for children and adults alike.*

 *Wonderful life lessons for all.*

Very enjoyable and true to our culture. (Akta Lakota Museum)

www.booksbycollins.com

THE BLACK CREEK MYSTERIES

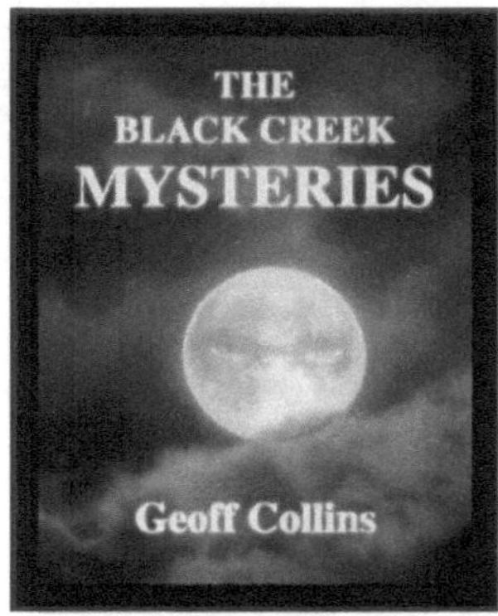

Alex Foster and Travis Sanders live in a small southern Ohio farm town named Rivers Edge. Their first adventure takes them to the remote desert town of Sunshine, Arizona, where they find themselves in the middle of the Legend of the Apache Death Cave. The following summer, after Alex and Travis graduate from high school, they head to the small fishing town of Black Creek, Maine, for a relaxing vacation before they both head off to college. Their trip becomes anything but relaxing when they discover a mysterious creature in an underwater cave and a network of deadly gunrunners.

www.booksbycollins.com

THE MERCY KILLINGS

 ***Holy City Mystery Artfully Spun***

Geoff Collins is a wonderfully versatile writer (check out his bibliography), and here, he weaves a delightful mystery set in the Holy City. Hop along and crack this case with Giordano—you won't regret, and it will get you primed for the other books coming along in the series.

Well Written...Interesting Characters and Plenty of Suspense

 Good mystery with interesting characters and plenty of suspense. A cybersecurity expert is hired to determine if narcotics theft is taking place at Charleston SC hospital and who is behind it. Well written with lots of fascinating details.

★★★★★ ***Wonderfully Crafted Story Set in Charleston***
Wonderfully crafted story set in Charleston, SC—great story line and vivid imagery. Collins follows Giordano with insight and honesty. Can't wait for Nick's next adventure.

★★★★★ ***A Fast and Exciting Read***
The book was a fast read. It was exciting and held my interest throughout. Hope to see more from this author.

www.booksbycollins.com

Reading Partners is a nonprofit literacy organization that recruits and trains community volunteers to provide one-on-one reading tutoring to students in under-resourced schools across the country. This highly effective program has helped thousands of children master the fundamental reading skills they need to succeed in school and beyond.

For more information, please visit www.readingpartners.org.

"Literacy is not a luxury; it is a right and a responsibility. If our world is to meet the challenges of the twenty-first century we must harness the energy and creativity of all our citizens."

—President Bill Clinton

www.ingramcontent.com/pod-product-compliance
Lightning Source LLC
Chambersburg PA
CBHW060542190726
48283CB00003B/831